T0070336

Personal PRISON

ANTINANA MIZU

authorHOUSE®

AuthorHouse™
1663 Liberty Drive
Bloomington, IN 47403
www.authorhouse.com
Phone: 1 (800) 839-8640

Published by AuthorHouse 10/16/2017

ISBN: 978-1-5462-1190-7 (sc)
ISBN: 978-1-5462-1189-1 (e)

The room was swimming in that quiet semi-darkness of the dawn. Dana couldn't sleep, she kept wriggling like a fish out of water, from side to side, and her thoughts were rustling in her head, exhausting her.

For some time now, in her mind persisted the idea that she would go mad among her colleagues with severe behavioural disorders. Yes, she will definitely become a lunatic, and the thought scared her awfully, it simply terrified her. At the present moment she wasn't blaming anybody anymore for her failed life (at least she thought so) as she used to do when she was in her states of deep depression. She was accusing her unknown parents, who had abandoned her, and thus she got among institutionalised children, she was accusing the staff, who sometimes ordered her authoritatively what to do and what to say, she was even blaming herself because she was having negative thoughts. They were thoughts that were crossing her mind, then vanished in thin air. It has been very hard to control them, make them melt ever since then, in their first phase. Her thoughts would catch shape amazingly fast, and she would fill with troubling feelings of guilt.

The girl sat upright and looked out of the window behind her. It had started snowing. Winter had come for some time, but there hadn't been any snow. Only cold, a terrible frost that penetrated you to the bone.

Dana was sleeping in a T-shirt and a pair of underpants. She slowly climbed down the wooden staircase of the bed, then he looked at the other girls.

She now felt some pity for them, although she had quite often considered them 'society's scumbags'. She actually included herself in this category, without any trace of pride. She had no roots, no home. She wanted to share joy, to feel her heart twitch with this feeling and wipe her tears in front of a gentle mother, who pities her and understands her pain.

There were only the stars' shadows left, the light traces had gone. The day had started to take shape.

Dana got out of her room, went towards the big windows in the hall and looked out.

It was 6.30 a.m. and the nurses had started turning up or leaving one by one, and although some of them greeted her, she went on looking out of the window, without answering them. These women had sometimes been hypocritical with her, had shown her a false love and a consolation as false (it couldn't be real love), and now she wasn't in the mood to say anything. Who could love her, no, women didn't nourish love, maybe some pity (sometimes).

She suddenly felt her armpits sweaty and headed with dragging steps towards the bathroom down the hall. She took off her T-shirt and underwear and got in the shower. The water was warmish, she felt how she was starting trembling and started rubbing herself. She couldn't stand stinking. It was something unpleasant. She would have stayed here forever, in the hall or even in the cold of the winter rather than have felt the pungent smell in the room, pills, blood.

Blood (when girls are on their periods) and the medical alcohol Ms. Boobs used to rub her armpits with. It is said that spirit ceased sweating and could even make underarm hair fall. Ms. Boobs actually hated washing herself, Ms. Boobs actually hated everybody. She was grudge-bearing and every time she wanted to smile there was a dumb grin, which revealed some nice teeth. Mrs. Boobs had nice teeth, and she didn't even realise that.

Dana had once beaten her up awfully. She had swollen her eye and broken her lip from which had flown plenty of blood. And that because Mrs. Boobs had been rude with her and had cursed her. Mrs. Boobs cursed everybody except Dana. Maybe her as well, but in an undertone. She was afraid of the girl, because 'she was strong and had a hard fist'.

Dana got out of the shower, and wet as she was, she put on her T-shirt and underwear again. She looked out of the window again and a sad smile appeared on her face. It was snowing, and in her soul there was no room for any joy. She was alone. Loneliness fastened her all over, as if it wanted to chain her forever.

She always wanted to seem strong, to scream out loud the desire of being a top spot, of even fighting windmills, but she didn't always succeed. She once cried a lot because she had lost her silver necklace, her one and only jewellery, given by Mario, the Italian who had come as a volunteer at the centre.

Maria was good-looking, with long hair tied in a pony tail at the back and eyes so blue that you felt like looking at the calm sea, no wrinkles at all. Mario liked her, took lots of photos with her and promised that she would also see Italy one day.

Dana was excited. And now Mario was sending postcards from sunny Sicily and lots of photos. Mario with a motorbike helmet, Mario smiling with a friend at the university. Mario in many snapshots. Dana couldn't forget him this way.

The Italian had become her far away friend, who brightened her soul whenever she remembered him.

It went on snowing outside, there was some snow on the stone slabs and Dana remained at the window near the hot radiator.

A woman touched her on her shoulder and she startled slightly.

'Hey, shortie, how are you? Why are up so early?'

Dana tried to put on a weak smile (it actually didn't look like a smile).

'Yes, I woke up because... well, just because... Why so many explanations?', mumbled the girl.

The nurse left with the impression of 'well, I actually don't even care about her', undulating her big bottom.

Dana then thought that a new day started, with a gloomy sky above, wrapped in that sordid monotony.

Breakfast in the morning, then, the girls anxiously waited for lunch and dinner. Otherwise, routine, routine, routine. And it was still all right, because one day, one humble day, she would be thrown out in the street and the rough and cold winter or the hot summer sun would whip her off carelessly.

She was just a nurse, namely the state allowed her to crawl just a little bit through life without having to beg in slimy clothes at the street corner or in the worst case, prostitute herself.

She had taken her hands to her temples as if she didn't want to think anymore or as if she wanted to stop the time. She could even picture herself opening her legs so that men could possess her wildly, with her head to one side, with her tears rolling on her cheeks and her jaw clenched in total agony.

For a second or two, she closed her eyes. She didn't exist for many, she didn't represent anything on earth, so nobody would hear her inner scream.

She entered the room, and her eyes were wet. She would succeed even if she had to cut off all the thistles beside the road, scratching her hands and legs. Her crowded life couldn't be so dark (she now believed this and cheered up a little bit).

Ms. Boobs was enjoying the milk powder with cocoa, talking loudly. The sun had risen on the icy sky. The grey above had magically disappeared.

Ms. Boobs took a small bite from a slice of bread with margarine, and threw it back loathingly on the plate.

'Well', she said loudly, 'what's with this dirt? These are not good. What are these stupid women giving us?', she nervously stroke the table.

'Hey, hey', screamed a kindergarten teacher, 'if you don't want it, nobody forces you. You may as well go on a diet, dear', Ms. Boobs went on objecting.

'This idiot country, with these idiot people', she mumbled in an undertone. She got up from the table, she knocked down the metal chair, and got out with her tripping walk.

'Pick up the chair', screamed a cook.

'Well, stupid', whispered Ms. Boobs.

The other girls started giggling, which otherwise never ever missed from the table. It was a sort of maintenance treatment, minutes of life which didn't simply fall apart, but somehow took shape. It was good to know that no girl was alone, everybody was on the same boat. All the girls (because it was a girls' dorm) could feel like they weren't alone and that they swam in waters that weren't as troubled.

Ms. Boobs went grumpily to her room and threw herself into her bed. 'What are they thinking?! Are they thinking I am stupid? They are the stupid ones, they are always giving us this miserable food.' The girl kept mumbling and she wasn't at least interested in the fact that nobody was listening to her.

She got under the blanket with her knees to her chest. She heard her stomach making noises, a sign that it rebelled against her own decision. 'Now, I won't be eating, not anymore, because they are dirt.'

'Don't you see that you are taking revenge on yourself?'asked Dana, entering with a plastic bottle, full of milk. For later, when she got hungry (there were three meals at fixed hours). The old carrot like-haired cook would take care of her and Dana always respected her for that.

Ms. Boobs stood upright as if electrocuted. Dana was her boss, and she was Dana's humble servant. How much she hated Dana for that! She was a villain, who didn't hesitate to take advantage of other people's weaknesses.

'Dana!', said Ms. Boobs, pushing the blanket aside and being able to stand in front of her boss.

'Listen, Bibi, you should have eaten first, and then you could have turned all tables upside down.' She put together a sly smile. 'Really, I wouldn't have been bothered the least bit. You were afarid of me, weren't you?'

Bibi nodded, and then she fixed her eyes on the floor.

Dana approached the girl who, even in her subconscious, considered herself a servant. A conditioned reflex had been formed.

Dana, the boss – her, Bianca Manole (her real name), the servant without any right of appeal.

She was called Ms. Boobs for her indecently big boobs, which raised, dangled like two bottles when she walked. And she never wore a bra. She used to wear one, ages ago, she got it from a girl from the centre she had been before. A pink bra, more to orange actually, and which Bibi tore in less than two weeks. The bra had already been worn-out when she got it. Since then she has decided not to wear one anymore. It was the best solution. In addition, she felt like she was being harnessed.

Dana sat on the bed and crossed her legs wearing immaculate white trainers. The girl was very clean and kept her belongings very tidily. Nothing she wore showed that she came from an orphanage.

'Bibi, come and see.' And Dana proudly took a thin silver necklace out of her blouse.

Ms. Boobs was looking with wide, amazed eyes.

'Oh', she said, as if she had just found a treasure, 'it's nice, yes, it's nice. Where have you got it from?'

Dana put it back in its place, the necklace sticking to her skin.

'It's a secret.' Then she said as if to herself:

'Do you know something? I am loved by lots of people'. Finally, she winked, and put out a sly smile.

'What is it? Do you want to sleep now?', she said as if coming to her senses, when she initially saw Ms. Boobs in bed.

The girl started stuttering.

'Well, eer...', she mumbled, 'it's cold'.

'OK, OK', said Dana laughing. 'But didn't you forget today's programme?'

'No, no', said Ms. Boobs, nodding firmly.

Micky, the Gypsy woman, was literally throwing flames on her nose.

'What?! Are you crazy, madam, have I stolen your make up?'

The woman, who was selling cheap make up on the market, had gotten ill-favoured because of her nerves.

'I saw you when you hid it in your pocket. Come on, show me your pockets.'

'Eeeh, you are crazy', shouted Micky, with her thick voice, because of the inhaled tobacco smoke.

The woman rushed to her and shook her soundly.

'I work, do you hear me? I work.' Her voice was hoarse and rough.

'Wait, wait', said the girl, trying to temper her aggression. 'Look, I didn't take anything', and she reversed her pockets. 'You're lying that you saw me hiding the box in my pocket. Did you think that you're going to trick me? It doesn't work. I won't give you money because I don't have any, and even if I had, I would still not give you any. You are disgusting!'

Micky left cursing. A stupid woman. She came from an orphanage, but she was not a thief.

Everybody had distorted opinions about her. And that may have been because she had a dark complexion, she couldn't hide it, she was a gypsy. She had become a phobia among the other people, the discrimination against gypsies. However, she was a pretty Gypsy, who had the right to life, who didn't need the crums that were thrown to her.

Micky burst into laughter, alone, in the street, thinking about this. How stupid, actually, she didn't even get the crums from anybody, unless she asked for them.

But she liked thinking like that, simply smiling to herself, at her own thoughts.

She was thinking she was beautiful and clever. What did she have to lose? She improved her mood and could laugh a little louder.

Micky was 20 years old, plump with big boobs (but not as big as those of Ms. Boobs), she would dye her hair bright red. She put a lot make up on her face, especially blue mascara and orange lipstick. Why orange? Well, because it was her favourite colour. She had orange training suits, T-shirts, and blouses, her trainers were the only ones of a different colour. They we given only black and white trainers at the orphanage.

She was walking on the pavement with her hands in her pockets and a smile stuck on her mouth. A car went past her very fast and splashed her with dirty snow, and she cursed loudly.

After a few seconds, she put on a smiley face again and thought that it was no use getting angry. Some people remained idiot and stupid and..., no matter what you did.

Micky had left from the centre with a leave note from

the manager. She had begged that woman with hair so tangled and grey as if she had hemp on her head.

The manager was a devilish woman, in any girl's opinion. She scolded her every time she didn't feel the need to defeat her aggression, to let the negativity inside her burst out.

And she wasn't going to be shouted at by anybody at all. Because nobody had ever fought for life like she had. When she was only five years old, her mother, a young and fat gypsy, had dragged her from the hut she called home, had taken her to an orphanage in Giurgiu. They actually lived in Giurgiu.

The memories were filtered through the fog of time, but in the girl's mind, they were somewhere in a corner of her brain, and they would have never melted.

On her way, her mother, the gypsy, told her in a loud voice, that she was just the product of a one-night wallowing in a stinking bed, which smelled like pee and other excrements.

'Your father was just an ordinary drunkard whom I wanted to f... that night... Are you listening to me or not? After that, I thought I shouldn't have. And look, you were born, a trouble on my head.'

Micky started crying loudly and her mother punched her strongly in the face.

'You, horrible gypsy, you! Would you like me to hold you?', she said spitefully, shaking the child. 'I don't know why I have kept you for so long.'

The little girl went on crying. Shouldn't children stay with their parents? Why did her mother reject her so fiercely? Had she never loved her?

'Why don't you want us both stay at home?'

The woman unveiled her yellow and decayed teeth, in a hidious grin.

'Home? Is that a home, you, bitter girl? Is that how you want to live? I'm offering you something better.' Then the woman shut up for a while, as if reflecting on something in order to save mankind. She finally whispered, looking away, in the distance. 'It is going to be all right. Yes, yes. You will have enough food to eat there.'

Walking slowly on the pavement, Micky thought now that there might be a little love for her in her mother's soul. The girl smiled sadly. She didn't care about anybody anymore. Not even about her mother, about whom she hadn't heard anything for 15 years. She might have been dead. The thought didn't cause any trembling. She wasn't interested.

She had stayed for about 7 years in the orphanage in Giurgiu and she would remember mostly the fierce cold during the winter nights, when the wet wood couldn't burn. Then, as if by magic, several children had been transferred to Bucharest and 'Flowers' centre had become her home. She had a place to stay, new colleagues, who considered her an intruder, but it was okay. She had heat in winter and a lot of good food.

Micky could survive anywhere. She was a fighter. Life had taught her how to fight and deepen knowledge about survival.

She would get beaten many times at the 'Flowers' until she mustered up her courage and started showing her true personality. She would throw herself into the fight. Didn't she happen to like this the most?

Doctoress Geta Popescu was looking on some medical records, deep in thought. What was she doing here, among crazy women? She thought all the women at the centre were crazy. They were taking everything for granted, all personnel had to do everything for them because they had been 'tricked' by fate.

The doctoress snorted and nodded. She had a miserable salary with which she had to support her 11-year-old son, Eduard. Her husband had left her two years before for a woman who was 10 years older than him. When he said farewell to her, she asked him for an explanation, with tears falling from her eyes, and him, and he looked at her with an involuntary, poorly camouflaged contempt.

'That's life, you can't ask too much if you don't have what to offer.'

What a mess! What did he mean by that, that she hadn't offered him anything, but mere crums? What a fool to imagine that woman was going to make his life a true heaven on earth!

She took a deep breath, then she exhaled slowly. Hey, why did she have to look into her mind, as if she was trying to suffer? Wasn't she seeking pain? Wasn't she thinking she was to blame for the fact that the scoundrel had left?

She shook her head and clenched her teeth.

God exists, Edy was with her, why should she have to worry?

'Doctoress, Ms. Boobs has broken a window and cut herself.'

The girl who put her head through the door had curly hair and lots of freckles. Her name was Stella and she desperately wanted to become a boy.

'Doctoress,' she said one day, 'I don't want to be tricked by boys. Please, you can operate on me, can't you?', and a foolish smile was widening on her childish face.

Geta assured her that it would be so, that she would become a true model of the hard sex.

And Stella would laugh and giggle like crazy.

'I'm going to beat all these pigs', she said raising her fist up like a winner, 'all these who have bullied me.'

She was waiting for the day when Doctoress Popescu would give her the big news: 'I'm going to operate on you now.'

At night, the dreams would repeat themselves compulsively.

They were about a handsome boy, he would glance boldly to beautiful girls in the street and he would suddenly find the perfect woman to have children with. She would wake up with a smile, her eyes shining due to an unexpected joy.

'What?'

The doctoress looked up from the papers.

'Ms. Boobs', repeated the girl, 'is out of her mind.'

The doctoress smiled weakly. Why did she also happen to be so sure of that? She had been working for two years at the centre and had seen so many things that nothing would make her tremble like it happened at the beginning.

Back then, she was taken over by fear. The girls would fight, pull their hair out. One of them had lost her teeth because of such a 'confrontation'. A masquerade, a cruel horrible joke.

'Yes, yes, Stella, I'm coming at once', hummed Geta.

She stood up slowly from the chair, and left accompanied by Stella to Ms. Boobs's room.

Taking advantage of the situation, Stella asked gentlely and softly like a warm spring breeze.

'When am I going to become a boy?'

Her smile widened on her face again.

'What? Oh, yes, one day.'

'When? When?', giggled Stella.

The doctoress leaned towards her.

'I'll tell you when the day is right'.

A crazy, crazy world.

Bianca Manole was kicking her bedroom's door. Dana was lying on her bed, looking at her as if she was watching an action film.

Her blood had drained on the carpet, the bad injury hurt her, but Bibi kept on expressing her aggression and screaming.

'Hey, you, stupid, hey, it hurts so badly!'

'Look at her', smiled Stella. 'She seems to have gone mad'. Then she left.

'Hey, Bibi,' said Doctoress Popescu conciliatorily. 'What happened?'

'Well, it hurts', whined Ms. Boobs.

The girl had broken the window on the hall and at the moment, the cleaning lady was picking up the splinters.

Geta tried to grab her by her arm and put her in bed, but the girl pulled her arm away.

'Leave me alone', she said and started crying. But at least she wasn't kicking the door.

'Bibi, Bibi, are you listening to me?' said the doctor. 'Lie in bed, I'll bandage your arm and it won't hurt anymore. Everything is going to be OK.'

The young woman finally lay in bed, cursing loudly.

The doctoress looked at the bad handwound, which was bleeding heavily. She went into the surgery and came back with some bandage and iodine.

'It'll burn', she said. 'I have to clean your wound. Come on, Bibi, be strong, you've always been strong, haven't you?'

Bibi clenched her teeth and, in response, spit a curse again.

'It hurts', she moaned.

'I believe you, Bibi.' Then, the woman slowly started cleaning her wound, while the girl was kicking. Again.

She would have liked to curse the doctoress, nasty Dana, everybody. She was really nervous.

'Calm down, Bibi', screamed Geta. 'If you can't stand pain, you should be calmer.'

'She should definitely replace some little wheels in her brain.'

'It hurts!', screamed Ms. Boobs as if from a snake's mouth. She had been sweating profusely, and she had wiped her forehead with the blood-stained T-shirt. Geta frowned for a few seconds. The wound was really bad. The cut was deep and it needed sewing.

She bandaged the girl, putting iodine first, and got out, and then came back after a few minutes.

'Bibi', she said, 'change your clothes, Dana, please, help her change her clothes, I have to go with her to the hospital.'

'No!', yelled Bibi, ' I don't want to go to those stinking hopsitals, where madmen swarm'.

'You went there for your head wound', said the doctress.

'You're lying, they gave me medicine, and I was sleeping like a log.'

She suddenly stood up, and with her healthy hand grabbed Geta by her arm.

'Am I crazy? Am I crazy?', and her eyes were sparkling just like a mad woman's eyes.

Geta licked her lips and sighed deeply. She tried to caress her head, but she rejected her.

'Tell me, don't you hear me?'

'No, you're not crazy', said Geta quietly, although her heart was beating mightily. 'They took you there because... because you didn't behave properly.'

'Not even now did I behave properly!', yelled Bibi. 'Do you hear me? Not even now. So, Hell', she said, and her eyes filled with tears. 'Rooms with greasy walls and lots of cockroaches'.

'No, Bibi, not this. Now you'll have your wound sewn and it'll be all. Then we'll go home.'

The girl breathed discontinuously with her eyes fixed on the ground. Then she whispered, as if to herself:

'No cockroaches, I want rooms with no cockroaches.'

Slowly, the darkness was covering the city like a molasses. But the trams, cars and buses were in a continuous back and forth. It looked tiring.

Ms. Boobs was leaning in her bed above Dana's.

'Does your arm still hurt?' Dana asked her, totally uninterested.

'No, it doesn't hurt me anymore...well... I thought they'd hold me at the hospital. You know, the cockroaches... the cockroaches.' Bibi seemed a child, just like that, with her fixed eyes, somewhere in the air soaked by different smells in the room.

'I know, Bibi', said Dana edgily, 'I know. And now, I'd like a little silence'.

Ms. Boobs didn't say anything and huddled, leaning her head against the wall. Wasn't she the humble servant and didn't she have to obey? Yes, she'll shut up and leave Dana with her own thoughts.

The other two roommates were out, Bibi wasn't sure where. So she had to stay near Dana so close, so alone as if she touched fear. She was afraid of Dana, maybe of her power to impose herself as a boss, and she, Ms. Boobs won't upset her, although... although what? Although she would have betrayed her, she would have hurt her, she would have knocked her down... She wished she saw her far away from her universe, of her difuse and maybe deformed world. But just like it was, with grey spots, Bibi thought it was her world.

She cuddled even more in the corner of the bed. She felt how cold was stinging her and she covered herself with the red quilt. She finally fell asleep, thinking of stars, which were likely to have appeared in the sky and were shining so brightly.

When she was little, Ms. Boobs used to admire the stars next to her mom outside. Both of them were looking towards the light.

Dana was tossing and turning from one side to the other and couldn't sleep. The room was swimming in darkness. Ms. Boobs had long fallen asleep, and Dana felt a strange repulsion against her. Bibi may have been quiet, comprised in a dream with many stars and a moon like a wax bun. She may have been all right, and she ... was tossing and turning anxiously waiting for the dawn. Nothing more unrelaxing.

The wind started blowing harder, she could hear its sound, like a bitter cry.

The girl's eyes suddenly filled up with tears. She felt so vulnerable, so helpless at that moment. Why was she waiting for daylight? Was she sometimes a villain? Why was she drowning in absurd pleasures? She felt as if her heart shrank with pain. She was nothing, because she was worth nothing, as a person. She knew she might upset God, she knew that, but why didn't she give up on everything? Why had she allied with human misery, what's more, why had she dropped it inside? She realised that rare were the moments when she was thinking just like she was then. Her mind was always soaked in abominations, and even though she was laughing like a lunatic, she seldom felt happiness.

Strangely, a few moments ago she felt pain, and now a strange joy (or maybe it wasn't strange?) No, this joy was actually seeded somewhere, like a small seed, in her soul. She now had the conscience of the sin. As if she had found herself all of a sudden.

She wished those moments froze in time, never metamorphose. But she was sure it couldn't be that way because she knew her own helplessness. Why did she have to think of her helplessness, why did her own thoughts unweave magic moments? Oh, God, she wished she slept. And she also felt that, the more they passed by, the seconds scattered the magic moments. The little part of joy went away, she was sinking into her inner self again, and who knows when it came out to lighten her being.

Ms. Boobs started snoring, and Dana covered her ears for a second, suddenly got up from her bed and felt how she was getting angry. She knew she was going to switch from one mood to another just as quickly as her thoughts were running in her head.

She cursed loudly and got up slamming the door. The hall was clothed in a dim light. She looked out of the window and saw that it was snowing again. Horrible. He really hated snow and blizzard, but she could hardly find a plausible explanation. The "cold" state probably caused her pain. Her inner child had always wanted heat.

Like that, with bare feet, she headed to the medical office. A nurse was always on duty. Dana knocked softly at the door.

'Maria?', she whispered. Maria was a nice young girl, who had got hired recently, and Dana liked her the minute she saw her. 'The others', she said, 'were shrews, who cared very little about the sufferings of the poor unfortunate women.'

'Come in', said the girl in a soft voice. She looked really sleepy and she was sipping from a big mug of black coffee to keep helself awake.

Dana sat on a chair in front of the young woman, who was sitting at the desk, on a swivel chair.

'You know', said Dana smiling, 'I'd like to be called Maria.' All her nervousness had miraculously disappeared as if a hot lava had crossed her body and infused a state of well being. Her eyes were shining softly, as if she entered a state of pure ecstasy.

'Do you mind my coming to talk to you?', Dana kept on smiling.

'No, how can you think something like that? But why aren't you sleeping?'

'Because, because...', Dana raised her eyes towards the ceiling, as if the white wall had written the answer, ' I don't want to waste my life', she finally said. 'You know, we go to bed, sleep like a log and what's in it for us? Nothing. We lose important moments from our life.' Maria sipped her coffee quietly, then said:

'We must rest, Dana, so that we can live. We can't really enjoy life without any rest. When you are rested, you can take everything from scratch. Have you ever thought that you see life from a different perspective in the morning, the sky seems clearer, even if there are heavy clouds above?'

'It isn't true', mumbled Dana. 'For me, everything is dark, I sink and see darkness.'

'But have you done anything to remove the darkness?'

Maria had found out about Dana's strange behaviour, about the white nights and the aggression crises. And she had also found something else, but not from reliable sources. She was somewhat afraid to even think about it. It was very hard to penetrate Dana's world, but not impossible. Maria really wanted that. It looked like a case study, but it wasn't. The woman really cared about the girls with so called serious behavioural disorders, whom she interacted with.

'Go to bed, Dana', she said softly. 'Tomorrow...'

'What tomorrow, Maria? Tomorrow I'll fight with all my strength so that another day goes by faster. And so on.'

'Go to bed', she repeated softly. 'Tomorrow it'll be fine.'

Dana strained her fists and felt a growing anger. She

switched from a state of apparent well-being to bad again. Tears pinched her eyes. Wasn't there anybody at all to really understand her? She had thought there would be.

'Why do you treat me like that, Maria?' Dana's voice was faint and somewhat serious. 'Why don't I get any bit of understanding from anybody? I need it so much.'

The nurse understood that the girl had taken it on a slippery slope. She stood up from the desk and came near her. She took her hand in hers, knowing the fact that she might be doing something really incautious.

'How could I not understand you, Dana? Who do you think I am? I don't want to upset you, that's all. I repeat, mornings can be very bright.'

'I've told you they can't!', screamed Dana.

'Yeah, right, right.' Maria took a deep breath. She no longer had anything to say, it seemed like her words had suddenly vanished as if flashed, how could she encourage a person who felt like collapsing? Was Dana really collapsing or had she always been like that? She might have begged a little affection when she was a child, she had needed it like air, and now, all that strong need had turned into aggression and a long and bitter depression.

Maria had read the girl's medical record. Dana had been abandoned in the hospital, her mother was only 17, and came from a good family. Then she found out from her colleagues that young girl had a relationship with her father's friend and had a child. She couldn't let her parents down by messing up thier lives with a newborn baby. As long as she was pregnant, the young girl stayed at her grandparents' house at the countryside. Her parents had sent her so that the girl wouldn't ruin their reputation.

Ruin their reputation? How stupid!

And Maria's thoughts started running through her mind as if wanting to find certain trajectories. Why had Dana's mother behaved like that? Why hadn't anybody understood her then? Why did she abandon the glimpse of life grown in her womb? Why couldn't she do anything herself for Dana?

Why do stars fall? Why does the Earth revolve? Why does the Sun heat the Earth?

Maria closed her eyes for a second as if she wanted to stop her thoughts. Too many 'why's, almost meaningless. Then, the woman opened her eyes and looked at the girl who was scanning the darkness beyond the clear windows.

'Come on', she said, 'we'll talk tomorrow.'

Dana murmured thoughtfully, as if for herself.

'Tomorrow, tomorrow...' and sighed loudly. 'I wish it were summer tomorrow and felt how the sun heated my body.'

Then she looked Maria straight in the eye. Her face twisted slightly.

'I need it so badly', she whispered as if he had clung to the last shred of hope. She bit her lips, then she burst into laughter.

'I'm going... I'm going to bed. Maybe, who knows, whatever you say, tomorrow the sky might seem clearer for me.'

She got up, smiling.

'What do you say? Is what I'm doing all right?'

Maria stood up.

'Do you want a pill? You'll fall asleep in a second.'

Dana nodded.

'Yes, I do want a pill. I want to sleep. Sleep a lot, look,

this is how much I want to sleep', she said, closing her eyes and moving her arms away. 'Sleep a lot, I mean a lot and never wake up', she emphasised.

The traffic was heavy, the vehicles were driving slowly because the snow had fallen in a very thick coat. Although the snow cleaning machines had worked all night long, everything was white and the streets were full of ice.

Ms. Boobs was ready. She was wearing a thick dark purple jacket, a thick training suit and brown ecological leather boots. She was also wearing a thick wool headband.

Dana looked at her smiling.

'Good job, Bibi', she said, gathering her knees to her chest. Then she looked towards the frozen windows.

'Come on, now go. It'll be fine.'

Ms. Boobs's laugh was so short as if it were a bark. She was very proud of herself now and she wasn't upset anymore because of the cut at her hand. If everything turned out just like Dana wanted, as well as she did, they might eat something better later in the evening.

Ms. Boobs thought that she didn't hate Dana that much that very second, even though she had done much harm to her. She sometimes taught her well, just like then, for instance.

'Come on, go!', screamed Dana, then her face suddenly changed, and her lips curled into a smile.

Ms. Boobs also smiled, and got out of the bedroom. She ran into Stella in the hall, the girl who wanted to be a boy.

'Bibi, Bibi', she said enthusiastically, 'I'll be a boy when the weather gets warmer. Hi, hi, hi', she laughed, uncovering her mouse-like teeth. 'This is how I'm going to fight with everybody', she said, straining her fists.

'You'll never be a boy, you, fool', barked Ms. Boobs to Stella. 'They're lying to you, and you believe them because your brain is as small as a pea.'

'It's you who has the brain the size of a pea', replied Stella and left gabbling. 'Could you just hear how stupid she is, I'll definitely be a boy', and started jumping from one foot to the other, joyfully.

'I'm going to be a boy, I'm going to be a boy, and I'm going to kick assess.'

Ms. Boobs went down the stairs, because her bedroom was upstairs, passed the big hall, smiled at the warden who wasn't paying attention to her, and went outside. For some time past, wardens didn't bother to ask girls for leave permits. Perhaps they were too much kept like birds in a cage.

Bibi smiled and threw a few glances along the thouroughfare that intersected with another.

So, everything was all right. There were lots of cars, and the traffic lights were close to the centre's gate.

Bibi hardly moved forward because of the ice that had formed on the stone slabs. A pale sun was shining in the grey sky.

A VW Passat stopped right next to the gate and Bibi, displaying, as usual, a stupid smile, rushed at the woman with the fur coat, who was getting out.

'Please, please', lamented Bibi, 'a penny, only a penny.'

The blonde-haired woman with the fur coat looked at her as if she were an intruder.

Seeing her face expression, Bibi asked.

'Am I asking too much, madam? Hi, hi, hi', she reacted

as if she were out of her mind. She was strange but a little funny, at the same time.

'Come on, madam', she insisted, and streched her hand, 'a penny'.

Bored, the woman searched through her handbag and took out a one-leu banknote.

'Here you are', she said. She wasn't used to giving away money to the beggars, but this girl had something special and cute and wasn't dump. She had always been impressed by the mentally ill, she even managed to shed a tear or two because of them.

Bibi thanked submissively and began the attack again. How proud will Dana be of her, maybe she'll appoint her deputy. Or, was she already the deputy? Dana was the boss, and she, Bibi Manole was coordinating the girls. Ms. Boobs lingered for a second, thinking, then, after a few seconds, said out loud:

'No, Dana is still their boss. Then, what am I?'

She shrugged her shoulders and kept on going. One day she'll think about that, too.

She kept on begging, building a face broken down because of suffering every single time. For a long time had she wanted to awaken something in people's hearts, a shred of mercy. After a while she saw how her pocket filled up with change. She didn't know how much she had gathered, Dana would count it carefully, then she would be thrilled.

Bibi grinned on her own and nodded. Dana would like the fact that she had 'picked up' some money, she repeated silently.

But later on, she had an unpleasant experience.

She saw a luxurious black car, without any trace of snow

on it and she rushed towards it, when it stopped at the traffic lights.

'Please', she babbled, streching a red hand.

The gipsy at the steering wheel opened the window, cursed her groasely and spit her between the eyes.

'Leave, bitch', he said through gritted teeth, and speeded up, splashing her with sleet.

Then anger lit in her eyes, and her lips started trembling a little. Strangely, she felt so embarrassed. No, that had never ever happened to her, Bianca Manole. People ignored her, threw disdainful looks at her, but they never made her kneel like she did now. Filthy gypsies! They saw themselves in a foreign car and all of a sudden had a gut as filthy as themselves, to think they were the centre of the universe!

She won't tell Dana and she'll keep on looking happy!

At the same time, Dana had a shower (she finally had hot water), she had washed her hair and she caught her hair in a ponytail. What was going on with Ms. Boobs? A smile bloomed on her lips. 'Who knows how she's begging. And she was doing it for her, her boss.'

Ms. Boobs kept on begging and putting the money in her chest pocket. She finally felt tired and even though it was cold outside, she felt very hot. Sweat wet her hair from her forehead.

'That's it, I think it's enough', she said in a loud voice, touching the full pocket with one hand and smiling foolishly.

The sun was setting slowly above the bustle of the city, a complex machinery which never seemed to stop. Ms. Boobs was starving, she hadn't eaten all day, she had just crunched some tasteless biscuits in the morning and drunk a mug of powder milk. But why did it matter? She touched her full pocket and a smile widened on her face.

The money she had gathered would make her happy, and with her slow mind she thought that Dana and she would eat a pizza that night. She loved pizza so much, and she licked her lips, besides, she hadn't eaten pizza for a long time. She thought, looking slightly up as if she were to find the answer there. It was summer, the sun was shining brightly, and she was standing outside the church, begging a whole day. How nice that she had met nice people and had gathered some money. She had put on a submissive face and remembered she had an injured hand, wrapped in a dirty mull. She had fought with a damn gypsy woman with a long dirty skirt. But she didn't remember why.

When she had gathered enough, then, in summer, Dana and she bought a lot of pizza and ate until they felt like fainting or worse, as if their bellies cracked.

Now, she was walking slowly, almost dragging her feet in her heavy thick boots, heading towards the centre.

The bulb at the entrance was casting a bright light, and Bibi smiled. She loved lights so much! She was afraid of the darkness, of the one outside and of the one inside her.

Bibi wasn't insane, but she couldn't be declared mentally healthy either. However, she had her moments of intense living, of strange lucidity, which she could use. She realised she sometimes indulged herself in a masochistic pleasure or she simply obeyed submissively, with tears in her eyes. She knew that she was weak and that she didn't have the power to rebel. She only rebelled against the personnel and the manager of the centre, but her head always bowed in front of Dana.

'Damn it', she sometimes cursed loudly. 'Why? Why had she become a slave, a puppy, who was waggiging her tail happily when Dana threw her a little bone?'

Now she was happy because Dana was happy.

She entered the orphanage building, grinned at the warden and climbed the stairs which led to her bedroom.

The girls were playing football upstairs. They had been given footballs by a foundation, and they were rushing in altogether to get one.

Ms. Boobs mumbled a greeting, stood still for a second watching them play, forgetting about the joy of seeing Dana again.

'Hey?', Stella, the curly black-haired girl, pulled her sleeve.

Seeing her, Bibi made faces, rolling her eyes.

'What else do you want? Did thet turn your pussy into a dick?'

'Stop laughing', said the girl slightly hurt, 'do you think I am talking nonsense?'

'No, no, how could I?'

'Tomorrow, I'm going to do my medical tests tomorrow. I'm going to be a boy', she emphasised, then she laughed heartily. 'What do you think?'

'Let me pass!'

'Bibi, Bibi, look', said the girl, with the voice strangled with excitement. She lifted her blouse, and squeezed her nipples from which gushed milk.

Bibi remained speechless with amazement, looking at her.

'What is this?'

'I don't know. It drips with milk when I pull my boobs. But the'll cut them off anyway.'

'You're crazy', said Bibi. Move away.' Why did she even care that it dripped with milk from Stella's boobs? So what? Her boss was waiting for her.

I'm seeing a doctor for this,' screamed Stella behind her. 'It sometimes hurts me.'

Dana was indeed waiting for her with a feverish impatience. She crouched in her bed just like a fetus in a matrix, with her thoughts far away, giving you the impression of indifference and coldness.

When Ms. Boobs entered happy and enthusiastic, Dana stood up lazily as if after a long white night.

'You finally came', she mumbled.

Then her voice became rigid.

'Why so long, Ms. Boobs? Do you think that you're playing with me?'

Bibi took a deep breath. She couldn't believe it. Didn't she starve all day long for her boss? Her boss's tone of voice scared her and that caused her a strange restlessness.

'Dana', she babbled, 'I, ... for you, ... for you..., I have...'

'Stop it', said Dana in a conciliatory tone, 'stop moaning, you stupid. I got angry. You see,' and an ironic smile crooked her face, 'I also have problems. Let's see what you've brought.'

Bibi started coughing until she got all red.

'L...look!', she said, panting. Her gibbersih hid a huge panic.

Dana took the money out of Ms. Boobs' hand, addressing her a feeble smile.

She weighed the money from one hand to the other, and a weak smile bloomed on her lips. She looked up and, seeing

Ms. Boobs' twisted face, who was standing with her hands behind, like a child, said:

'I'm done with his face which asks for slapping', she said conciliatorily. I have my own madness just as you have yours.'

Then she pushed away as if 'keep calm, I still consider you my accomplice. We're a team, but I'm still the boss.'

Later, Bibi went to buy a pizza (just like she hoped she would), lots of peanuts and orange juice.

She had a real treat, together with Dana and Micky, the gypsy they called later.

'This pizza is worth a whole day of hard work', thought Bibi. There will come a day Micky begs for her as well, but especially for Dana. Because all of them had to fulfil Dana's will.

The girl didn't seem to be older than 13. However, she was well-built, big elastic boobs, abundant pubic hair. It was dark because all the blinds had been pulled down, a dense coarse darkness.

The girl undressed slowly, under Dana's eyes. She kept biting her lower lip from time to time, sign of a weak unconscious excitement. She didn't dare look at Dana, see her look, sparkling like a flame. Maybe she also had burning eyes, but the girl didn't realise that. She didn't do anything but 'fulfil' what Dana had told her to do.

'You're undressing slowly, Nina, I want to see your pussy and your boobs. You'll feel fine, you'll see.'

Nina couldn't refuse her, because Dana had done a lot for her. She had bought her a necklace from the market, then a bracelet and had given her lots of sweets. Dana had lots of sweets, and Nina had no idea where they came from. At the orphanage they were rarely given a cake or a candy. In conclusion, she didn't care, but still... She gave in to questions and excesses of curiosity.

Now Nina was naked in front of Dana. She was leaning against the wall and looked like a slut who was waiting for her client with hidden embarrassment.

She stayed like that for a few seconds or minutes, she didn't know how many, she felt like time had frozen, as if waiting for a new beginning. She didn't feel any embarrassment. She had stood naked many times in front of her colleagues in the bathroom or when they put on their pyjamas at night. But she never undressed in front of Dana. One day, she said that she cared for her, held her tight and caressed her on her head. Nina felt attached to her, considering her the elder sister she had never had or her lost mother.

Generally, at the orphanage, the girls fought with one another, pulled their hair out or bruised one another's eyes, sign of a poor education and not having a good start in life.

'What, err... she doesn't help Dana with anything but she still has everything', said Ms. Boobs out loud one day at the entrance hall. Luckily, Dana didn't hear her, or if she did, she pretended not to. Ms. Boobs' reaction might be normal, but Dana couldn't give her anything from what she wanted to give Nina. Nina was fragile, naive and very cute. Her smile lit her face and her black eyes like two beads sparkled. Her soul was clean.

The girl looked up slowly, her eyes being focused so far on the floor covered with a green mat.

Dana stood near the door, dressed up in an incredibly clean training suit and white trainers, just as clean. Dana never got dirty. Her hands were stuck in her trousers' pockets. She would wear her hair in a ponytail.

At the moment, she wasn't thinking of anything else but how beautiful Nina's body was. And her wavy, ebony shoulder-long hair. She was beautiful, the most beautiful girl of the orphanage. She still remembered that summer day when the little girl came accompanied by a social assistant with shaggy hair.

It was so hot, the bright sun had melted the asphalt, and Nina had beads of sweat on her forehead. Her mom and dad were jailed for drug trafficking. Nobody knew when their sentence was over, and they crossed the threshold of the tall gates, towards freedom.

It had been 5 years since Nina came to the orphanage and Dana realised that she had got attached to her since then. A lonely little girl, secluded, as if earnestly asking for protection. As long as she is in the orphanage, nothing bad will ever happen to Nina.

Once, a nurse wanted to give her a pill, because Nina was crying out loud, almost without any reason (at least that was what the nurse had thought, but the girl actually missed her parents). She was going to forget them afterwards.

When the woman came with the glass of water and the pill, Dana slapped her hand nervously, broke the glass and hurt the nurse.

'She doesn't need the pill', screamed Dana, 'she isn't crazy like us. She is crying for a reason, she just needs...' She hesitated for a moment and then said:

'She needs me.'

She seemed like a lioness ready to protect her cub no matter what. Then, at that time, she was thinking of Nina only as a child who must be protected, and who desperately wanted to fill the emptiness in her soul. And also at that time, Nina was only a child, without any body forms.

It all started a year ago. Her boobs got bigger, enough to be caressed, and her pubic hair was short and rough.

Dana had washed Nina many times when she was a child, but for a year now, she hasn't wanted that. She knew her weakness trembling within her. She hadn't seen her naked for a year, since the fantasies appeared in her mind.

Yes, and now her weakness persisted within her, making her helpless, squeezing her any thought that might have brought feeelings of guilt. She didn't want anything bad to happen to Nina, but still, she indulged (and she knew that) in a dirty situation. The world was insane, and she was revolving in a carousel of madness, just like this, left, right, left, right.

Now all Dana wanted was to touch Nina, touch her naked boobs, and feel the warmth of her body. Nina looked at her intensely, slightly reserved, but without too much embarrassment. Dana had taken her clothes off with her own hand many times, and a sincere smile outlined her lips. Why was she ashamed now? Nina couldn't realise many things nor read too much in her protectress's greedy look. She was a child who had lost a lot in her lifetime, maybe her childhood itself. She had grown up together with her parents who injected themselves white poison and easily forgot about her. Seconds passed one after the other, minutes, hours, but they couldn't wake up from that numbness which was uglier than death.

The greasy flat was sometimes full with greasy people, who laughed viciously and loudly. Their and Nina's parents' laughter broke through the air, defying even the silence of the nights.

Dana came close to her, streching her hands, and the girl giggled.

'Dana, you love me, don't you?' laughed Nina, looking into the young woman's eyes. It seemed like a mild fear blossomed in her soul, but she didn't realise that. Never ever would Dana hurt her. Dana loved her as much as she loved Dana.

Dana's eyes were swimming in withheld tears. She also felt fear. What would happen next? Her lips slightly half-opened. Her head became completely empty of thoughts. It was just Nina, the child, wrapped in the whiteness typical of purity. It was just her Nina.

She almost whispered without realising:

'I love you, Nina.'

All the evil in the young woman's soul were gone. The aggression and restlessness were gone. The selfishness and envy were gone. For Nina (and she felt it that very moment), she would have gladly sacrificed her life, which she wouldn't have done for anybody else.

She came much closer to the girl, and she finally held her in her arms. Scalding tears fell down her cheeks.

'Oh, Nina, my little girl, I am lonely, so lonely. Your mommy is lonely. Don't you want to help me?'

The little girl shook her head affirmatively. She would always help her Dana, she would have done anything for her.

She was holding her tighter and tighter.

'Be close, be close to me, my little girl. Nothing will break us up. I have been waiting for this for ages.'

Dana covered the child's face, her shining eyes, cheeks, lips slowly with gentle, maybe slightly passionate kisses. She gently touched these last ones, without thinking about anything. And that was because there was a possibility that the feeling of guilt could disturb the great excitement she was feeling now.

Next, she fell on her knees and kissed her legs, from the upper side from the hips to the heels, as if feeling a pleasant agony from which she didn't want to wake up. Nina's toes were small and scattered, like those of a child. Dana touched them softly with her lips, her hot breath warming them up. Nina was looking down, towards her friend and protectress in a silent excitement. She liked this game, she hadn't played it with anybody before. And she loved Dana so much. She made her feel so good.

Dana finally collapsed on the floor. With her head on one side, she whispered:

'Get dressed, Nina.'

The little girl huddled near the young woman. She moved her lips, and her heart started beating mightily. She would have never wanted to upset Dana.

'Have I done something wrong?', she babbled.

Dana's lips crouched in a smile.

'You never do anything wrong, I … always do.'

'Why?'

Dana got up slowly, and sat on her buttom. She caressed the girl's face, which was red like fire.

'Adults always make mistakes, my baby. They make

mistakes after mistakes. Some regret them, others find explanations, absurd, meaningless excuses.'

She shut up for a little while and then said, starin at the snow which just started to fall, beyond the frozen windows.

'I really want you to get dressed, honey. And...', she held the girl with both hands, looked her in the eye ... 'forget that tonight ever existed.'

She might have gone further if she hadn't heard the scream within her, imaginary but so threatening. She might have deflowered the little girl with her finger and would have laughed like crazy when her blood had spotted her hands. She was pathetic. She didn't deserve anything from life, not even a small grain of joy. She couldn't think of happiness anymore because she couldn't aspire to such a special feeling.

The dense darkness flooded the room. Ms. Boobs was sleepingd snoring like an animal. The other girls were sleeping quietly.

Dana lit a cigarette, although it was against the rules of the orphanage (you could smoke outside or in the special designated areas for smoking).

Was she really insane? But the scream was so real that it seemed it would break her eardrums. Otherwise she wouldn't have stopped from her sin. She was sitting up, with her legs stretched, and she was smoking quietly.

Did she like women? Did she like children? Did she like men? Was she a lesbian? Was she a pedophile? Was she a bisexual?

Too many questions, she had a headache. She had to analyse herself, to get to know herself better. Maybe she didn't know what lay within her. She finished smoking, and threw the cigarette butt out of the window. Yes, she liked Maria, the nurse, but just as simple she might like her, too. What, can't girls like each other? Can't they make friends anymore? That doesn't mean she is a lesbian. No, she wasn't a lesbian. At least that's how she felt at the time being. Otherwise, she couldn't have liked Mario, the Italian so much, the guy who had sent photos. She could be bisexual, why this outburst for a year, why these fantasies about Nina, who was a child, after all. Could she be considered one of those miserable pedophiles? Maybe they were mentally ill and emotionally unstable. But what could she say about the abused children? She didn't accuse the pedophiles, but how about their victims, whose chilhood is basically taken away?

She felt fear with regard to her own feelings. Will there come a day when she makes Nina suffer? She shook her head vertiginously. No, no, God, no. Maybe the dark side within her wanted that, wanted the sin, and could get that some day. How could the bright side fight back? Were there within her more lights than shadows or vice versa? One thing was for sure, she was a miserable woman. And that was because she didn't make any effort whatsoever so that the shadow within her would shrink. She would never remove all of it, otherwise she would have entirely been covered in light and would have become a saint. Nobody, not a single human being on this planet was a saint. There wasn't anybody without any sins. She smiled bitterly. And she didn't want that. She just wanted to be an average person. But what did average really mean and within what limits did it fit?

A person, a thing might as well be considered normal for some, and abnormal for others. That was known for ages.

Dana couldn't sleep. She lit one more cigarette, not being interested in the fact that there was a dense smoke in the room, which could have bothered the girls.

Ms. Boobs had stopped snoring. She tossed from one side to the other and munched, slowly sniffing the sour smell.

'Hm', she crooked her nose, 'I can't breathe.'

'Just sleep!', said Dana with a rough voice. That was the last straw, Ms. Boobs's rebellion. Didn't she have enough problems? She was actually struggling not to go mad. Or had she already gone mad?

'Hey, hey', her own thoughts calmed her down, 'don't take it like that anymore.'

Then it was her again who thought that it would be nice if she tried to sleep at that moment. She would forget everything in a few hours. She would know what to do in the morning. She threw the cigarette out of the window, pulled the pillow as comfortably as she could, put her head on it and covered herself with the blanket.

Her eyes were closed, and her lips were saying the Lord's Prayer.

Ms. Boobs goggled, her eyes were troubled and wide open as if there were a real monster in front of her.

'Would you stop looking at me like that, like a fool?', shouted the man.

'Err.. this is my house.'

'Sure', he grinned maliciously. Then, she came closer to her aggressively,

looking her into the eye like a mad man.

'You'll stay here', he said and pointed his index finger towards the floor. 'You're nothing but a worm, which only comes out to light when it rains. A miserable worm, which crawls through filthy hostels. You'll sign that paper! I've got children.'

Bibi started crying slowly, eyes on the ground. It was her house, inherited from her parents who died because of a car accident.

Back then, a long time ago, when she was only 7 years old, she wept bitterly on Uncle Joe's shoulder, who now turned into a real enemy. He had got married for a while, and his wife gave birth to three children.

He pulled out her hair when she told him she was pregnant with the third one.

'Are you out of your mind?', he screamed like crazy. 'We live in a box of matches, and we pay lots of money on rent.' He pushed her away with his strong hands on the hard bed where they had usually had sex. Lots of sex, Joe wanted lots of sex.

'I'll lose the baby', babbled the woman, with tears in her eyes.

'Ha, ha, ha', laughed Joe, exalting at the thought itself. 'One mouth less to feed.'

Then his eyes narrowed like two threatening brown cracks.

'You'll have an abortion, do you hear me, woman?'

But the woman didn't and came up with a brilliant idea.

'We can have a big house, baby', she suddenly said, with a sly smile in the corner of her mouth.

Her husband's facial traits changed, gaining that mixture of astonishment and inquiry.

'How?', he mumbled. His index finger was caressing his unshaven cheek.

'You see, you poor brother, Nelu, May God rest his soul, had a big house, we would all fit in there...'

'Well...'

'Wait', she said, putting two fingers on Joe's lips. 'I know, it belongs to Bianca, his daughter, but she's crazy, she's really dump, and she gets government help. All you have to do is make her give it to you, by signature.'

Joe thought about it for a day or two. He thought about it even at night, until he made up his mind. His wife was right, he could take hold of the house if Bianca wanted, and then the money for rent were going to be spent on food and his family, and he was going to live a better life.

But... (for a few moments, the feeling of guilt stung him) the girl would remain homeless. He'd never let her stay with him. And that was because she was slovenly and stupid.

When his brother and sister-in-law died, he showed affection to the little girl in pretense, he let her cry her sorrow on his shoulder, but he never loved her. She had been ugly ever since she was little. After Bianca's parents' funeral, Joe didn't need much persuading (and because he was her only relative), he took her to an orphanage. He had to get married and have children.

Still, to take away her house... might be too much. Back then, in the past, when he had let her at the orphanage, he swore he would come back and take her. He caressed her on her head and left, coming back after 5 years when the girl turned 12, then he completely forgot about her until now.

'Listen, woman, I don't know if Bianca is going to give

me her house. I left her for such a long time. She may be able to live alone now.'

The woman screamed like crazy.

'Don't you understand she's insane? She was hospitalised as a fruitcake.'

'Fruitcake?'

'Yes, out of her mind. Why do you wonder? How do I know? I've asked around. Do you think that I got this idea so suddenly? And why do you think I kept the baby? Because we are given a great chance, do you hear me?'

I went once or twice at the orphanage, I don't know'. The woman calmed down a little and tempered her voice. 'I got her something to eat, I left it to the guard, he was a very kind boy. I showed him my ID, the same surname, I told him I was her aunt, and he told me lots of stories. As I told you, the girl was hospitalised at the madhouse many times. She is said to have behavioural disorders.'

'She won't give up the house', said Joe deep in thought. The woman's face turned red from anger.

'That's what you say,' she groaned. Then, with a gentle face, she lay on the bed and tried to shed a tear.

'You don't want the baby, that's it.'

Joe didn't know what to say. He didn't really want the third child. He was already breaking his back working on the site for these two. His wife didn't work. Joe knew she was lazy but someone had to take care of the children as well.

'I want the baby', he lied.

She pretented to believe him, although he had been violent a few minutes ago.

'Baby, baby', she clung to him like a liana. She pressed

her lips on his forehead. 'You're wonderful! Are you going to go to that stupid girl?'

And Joe nodded, because he also liked the idea, and Bianca was really stupid, she resembled her father. He also used to be stupid, as well as his wife. A family of stupid people.

Seeing her now, his beliefs strengthened. The girl looked horrible. She was dirty, she smelled awfully of sweat, rare and bleached hair like a broom. Not that he was the embodied cleanliness, he rarely washed himself, but the girl was really filthy. But she had huge boobs (they were pretty obvious).

They were standing in the hall, upstairs, where Bibi had her room. Hearing a man's loud voice, three or four girls came closer, looking curiously at them.

Joe glanced at them, then said with a voice choked with anger:

'You know what, let's go somewhere.'

'Err, why?'

He raised his hands up in the air, looking desperate.

'To... talk.' He stressed the last words which came out of his mouth hissing. 'There are some curious girls here who don't know what they want.' He looked threateningly at the girls, and Bibi turned around, and with an unusually calm voice, begged them to leave. The girls left without further comments. Bibi was next after Dana in that miserable orphanage (but Bibi didn't know that).

Joe tried to come up with a smile, but he only managed to put on a pitiful grin. What should he do now, mime a feeling of great love, wallow on the floor like a dog? He needed the house for him and his family. His third child had just been born, Lena, a fat and gluttonous baby girl. Joe smiled goofily thinking about her. He was going to love her after all, even if he didn't want her at first. Now he had to try the impossible with this miserable niece of his.

'Would you mind listening to me a bit, little girl?'

Bibi smiled broadly, enough to make Joe go out of his mind.

'Listen, why don't you want to sign?'

'I don't want to give you the house.'

'Idiot woman', thought Joe.

'Why?'

'Maybe, some day', and Bibi looked dreamily towards the ceiling, 'I'll leave this place, I'll leave', she emphasised these words and turned towards her uncle, 'and I'll live in my house.'

'Hm', said Joe sarcastically. 'Not everything that glitters is gold, sweetie.' 'Then', he said, knowing that the girl wouldn't understand his proverb, 'you're going to live with me, your aunt and cousins.'

He wondered what his wife would do, and was aware of that strange panic deep down in his mind. He loved his wife, and she knew how to subjugate him enough to have him at her feet. All in all, she was the boss, even though he hit her from time to time. Because of the anger, daily stress, thought Joe. And now he was too stressed because of this stupid girl. He kind of lost his patience and knew the fact that if the girl mastered the situation, he would slap her. And he would have really liked to hurt that dumb face, but then she would become more stubborn.

'Joe, don't be stupid, you can't lose something you haven't even won yet', thought the man. He took a deep breath and calmed down a little.

'Listen to me, for your sake.' He caressed her head with one hand, with his fingers ready to smash her skull.

'It is going to be all right, all of us are going to be all right', said Joe with his mouth distorted in a sly smile.

'Leave!', Bianca burst out. Her eyebrows frowned threateningly.

Joe was slightly shaking. He moistened his lips with his tongue.

'Fine, I'm leaving.' His lips narrowed so much that they looked like a stripe.

'I'll come by again to talk. And look' (he took out from his coat's pocket a lollipop), take this. It's really good.'

'Leave!', screamed Bibi and bitter tears were shining in her eyes.

Joe left and thought that he showed 'complete understanding' towards his niece.

'Damn bitch', he whispered down the stairs.

Bibi felt fear close to horror. She didn't understand too much, things got troubled, but this man wanted something she cared about a lot. It was the house where she had grown up together with her dear parents. She barely remembered, due to the foggy memories, how her mother used to heat the milk before bedtime and held her tight with tears in her eyes. Bibi didn't understand why her mother had tears in her eyes whenever she looked at her. She had been a sensitive child who would become a sensitive, maybe troubled teenager. She remembered that she also took pills back then, which she swallowed like candies.

Bibi knew that she had now become a troubled adult.

Deep inside her confused mind, she could realise that. Maybe her mother knew that some day the fire that was smoldering in her daughter's brain would eventually break out.

'I'm sorry, mom,' she whispered and her mind seemed sharper than ever.

She was standing in the hall and her tears were falling, washing her face. The radiators were burning, and Bibi leaned on one, looking unbalanced through the double glazed barred window. Would this be her place forever? No, because after a short while they would throw her in the street. She was passed a certain age when the state assumed responsibilty.

What would become of her? A dumb smile appeared on her lips. She'd go to her house.

Her house, which Joe wanted to take it away from her. They'd live together. Damn! Who did that asshole with a crooked nose and small pig-like eyes think he was?

Joe, the madman, Joe, the pitiless. Joe gathered the evil. Joe and Dana. They sometimes seemed to resemble one another. She didn't know which the common points were, but Joe and Dana resembled one another. Maybe they were both evil.

Bibi looked outside for a while. The warden was opening the doors of the bread delivery vehicle, Skippy the dog was feeding her puppies whom she had given birth a week before, one or two nurses were taking the laundry to the washhouse.

The same view Bibi was sick and tired of, like an old coat which had to be thrown away.

She suddenly felt a furious tension, which started to squeeze her slowly like a vice.

She kicked the floor tile and cursed loudly. The calm

that had wrapped her a while ago had vanished like magic. Bibi was just like that, that was her temper. She could go from one mood to another very easily, as if she dove from the ground into the water, no holds barred.

'Damn it', she screamed, 'err.. what, is this entire world crazy?'

She looked directly towards the window from the door which had just been put there, her eyes were shining brightly, then she looked at her bandaged hand. That was what she wanted now, that was what she felt instinctively, to break the window again. She thought a bit, for only a second or two. She'd feel pain again and the worst that could happen could be that they would take her to the madhouse again, where they would give her lots of pills. And she didn't want that.

Her lips started shaking, as if she was staying in an icy room. Her fists were clenched, as if ready for an imaginary fight. She was standing like a statue waiting for a signal to fight.

Maria, the nurse, dressed in white, passed by her with a box full of pills. She stopped when seeing Ms. Boobs's contorted face.

'Bibi?', she came closer, looked her in the eye and put a hand on her shoulder.

'Did something happen, Bibi?'

Of course something had happened, these girls can never be calm, their minds knead dozens of ideas, of certaind shades.

Bibi pretented not to hear her, then she removed the woman's hand.

'Leave, take care of your stupid girls.' She threw a mean, icy cold look to Maria. Her lips curved, showing sarcasm.

'You are all the same, you from the < normal world>. I, I,' said Bibi agitated and pointing with her index finger to her chest, 'I am nothing but a mere cloth on which you wipe your feet. You, you, who...'

She seemed to be choking and her eyes filled up with tears again. Maria felt like something had happened. She tried to feel the ground without the mines exploding.

'Would like to come to my office and talk, Bibi?'

'No... I don't think so. Why?'

'I'd like to try, just give it a try to change your opinion about yourself.'

'What would you like?'

'I'd like to tell you that you're not like you think you are. You are a normal person.'

Bianca's tears dried on her cheeks.

'Listen', she said, moistening her lips with her tongue, 'I know what I am. I've got isssues and you know it very well, don't lie to me anymore.'

Maria retreated and sighed.

'Fine, suit yourself, but you should know that I have issues, too. Everybody has. But do you know what is most important? Never give up the fight.'

Maria knew very well how aggressive Bianca could become. Her restlessness merged with her aggression and made up an explosive mixture. The girl was mentally ill, but someone had to explain to her that it was not that bad so that she could grant herself attenuating circumstances.

'I'm crazy, I'm responsible for my deeds. I can commit murder, I just don't want them to isolate me in that shell with really small iron windows. I'm Ms. Boobs and you should pay attention to me.'

No. That was definitely not what the girls should believe. They should look inside themselves and feel like they were not insane. They only have mental problems, which cannot always be so close to madness. Maybe a little retardation.

Maria was about to leave, when Bibi grabbed her arm.

'You're a good girl.'

Maria smiled.

'Do you think so?'

'Yes, forgive me.'

'Do you promise me you'll be a good girl?'

'Yeah, I don't know.'

'OK', laughed Maria, knowing that Bibi could never be too 'good'. 'And let me tell you something. I think that today something happened that made you uunhappy, but when you need help, I don't know, as much as I can, call me.'

The dawn trickled down the drawn blinds. It was freezing cold, which got her paralysed, even though it was warm inside. Dana stood up and rubbed her naked arms. The dream. That must have been it. She had dreamt that she was swimming in icy cold water, a blackish shadow was hovering above her and she was too weak to remove it. The light within her being was gone, had vanished in thin air, and her shadow seemed to show its claws. Did the shadow have claws? She didn't know that very well.

The icy cold water in her dream seemed to make her tremble even now, the moment she was awake.

'I don't want to dream anymore', whispered Dana. 'I don't want mud and horror around me'.

She got out of bed, as she often did when her soul shook with restlessness and went to the bathroom.

She switched on the taps and... what a miracle! There was hot water running. It was all she needed after the rough cold from the previous night.

She took off her clothes, then got into the shower and let the hot water wash her body... It was good, so good and it seemed that her thoughts suddenly stopped torturing her. The water was running abundently, and she got more and more serene. She stood more than fifteen minutes under the hot water, so that her skin turned red. She got out, switched off the taps and span around in the thick green towel which she had taken from the room. She looked out of the window. It had stopped snowing. The sun might try to shine. A weak smile brightened the girl's face. It would be all right, she knew that, it would be all right.

'Try being what you are, what you want to be, not what others want you to be', said an old woman to Micky once.

'Try being what you are, what you want to be.' Micky was sitting on the old frayed armchair with a finger in her mouth, thinking.

'What did she want to be?' ... She wanted... what did she want? A house where she lived with her boyfriend, lots of money and she didn't want to live in the orphanage anymore.

Micky thought for a few minutes, biting her thumb nail.

The old woman didn't want to tell her that.

'Try being what you are.' Her mind and heart shouldn't be influenced by others. Oh, it was pretty hard to understand, but perhaps that was it. Try telling the truth even if it hurts. Often had she told the truth and she got into trouble. Since then she had been trying to dimish it and let lie loose.

She was Micky, she was gypsy, but she didn't let anybody put her down, nor her personality.

Once, there came a young girl to see Dana. She was gypsy, with dark complexion and very muscular. Dana had her fight with Micky (knowing that she had heavy arms).

Micky and Tea (that was the gypsy's name) had a terrible fight like two tigresses. Tea proved to be stronger, so Micky got a broken nose, a sprained hand and a bad behaviour report. Another two or three of those and she would sleep under the stars.

Could she sacrifice herself for Dana? Did everything have to revolve around her?

Micky knew Dana wasn't bad, she enjoyed it too much pretending to be the boss and having fun.

Then, during the fight, Dana stood and watched, clapped her hands and laughed out loud.

Micky sighed. Will someone ever punish Dana? Because, sometimes, unwittingly, Mickey fiercely wanted something bad to happen to the girl, and said 'there will come a day when she will suffer and everything around her will collapse'. She really hoped that.

Then, when the mood changed, she would wake up thinking about Dana with excessive sympathy.

'Poor Dana, she's alone, she really doesn't have anybody, not even a boyfriend.'

Micky lit a cheap cigarette and spread the sour smoke towards the ceiling. She enjoyed the pungent odour for a moment or two, without thinking about anything. Then she looked around the room. The walls were shriveled, full of mould, you could barely see the dirty violet colour.

A stinking bed, lying in the middle of the room, a plastic table, three chairs, an old black and white TV set (which had broken down several times) and a cooker as old.

This place was rightfully her real nest.

A smile fluttered on her lips. She remembered the day when she met Tom.

It was in summer, in July, a hot sun was heating the earth and Micky went to the pool. She had a bright orange swimsuit which she was proud of. She saved every single penny to buy it.

She was alone, lying on the mat, on the fresh grass, near the lake. She lit a cigarette, leaning on her elbows. He had been looking at her closely for a while. The girl was beautiful, and as dark-skinned as he was. He went to her to light his cigarette.

She smiled, exposing her yellow teeth. Hey, he was hardly Prince Charming riding on a white horse. Why so much excitement?

With lazy gestures, she reached out her cigarette so that he could light his. He thanked her and asked her if he could sit next to her. 'I'm also alone', he said and let her understand whatever she pleased. Was he alone at the pool or in this futile world?

Maybe both. She let him sit next to her on the mat and she felt that she wouldn't get scared at all, for the very first time in her life. She was used to getting into conversation with strangers, but with a certain fear attempt. She couldn't get inside their minds and wasn't able at least to read people's faces. But now it seemed that she had read his soul, just like that, just in a few minutes. She realised her eyes were gentle and couldn't hide trash.

They became friends soon, and when leaving, he kissed her on the cheek, and she shuddered. An unexpected excitement invaded her. He looked for her at the orphanage the next day (she told him she was a mere orphan girl in an orphanage), and he just settled for a shoulder shrug and a weak smile.

What did that mean? She didn't think too much and took the bright side of things. He wasn't interested. She had the proof the next day, when he came to see her.

'You're beautiful', he said with a warm and manly voice, even though he was just a 22-year-old boy.

'And I want to see you every day.'

Micky exposed her teeth again. Her heart started beating crazily. 'You're beautiful', he said. She was very glad when she heard that and she was happy and glad about what she looked like. She always liked to show off her shapes, to feel good about her looks, to look good. She always hoped to find her Prince Charming, who would take her away from the orphanage which smelled like mould. And that was because it creaked from eveywhere. There were pain, humiliation, human misery there.

Tom took her at this house after a week. Micky made love for the very first time in her life, and he was completely amazed that she was still a virgin. He had never met a virgin before.

And he began to love her little by little.

Micky finished smoking the cigarette, and crushed the cigarette butt in the ashtray. She watched TV for at least half an hour (an old film, whose name she had forgotten), then Tom came.

He had bought a cheeseburger with lots of sauce, mustard and a big bottle of coke.

That night, Mickey will be all his. They made love so many times that they were both sweated profusely.

Everything would have been perfect if he could support her financially, get married and be able to start a family.

Tom came from a broken home, with several moms and dads, blood brothers and stepbrothers, he didn't know too much about it, either.

He just lived for the present, together with Micky and dreamed about his future with her, too (even though he was just a hodman, and the crib where he lived was just rented).

He wanted to take the girl away from the orphanage, where, not for long, if she didn't find a job, she'd be thrown out.

Micky neved told him about Dana. The girl was a bit afraid at the thought that she had to reveal someone (even her boyfriend) what life was like together with Dana or Ms. Boobs. All the girls were Dana's servants, and even though she sometimes didn't like it too much, she often indulged herself in that game (it was a game, after all, of humiliation and pleasure). Her thoughts sometimes went crazy, reason disappeared, and she let herself in the mercy of fate. She often liked to feel pain. A vertiginous excitement invaded her and the screams that detached from her lips were rather pleasure. In fact, the screams mixed with laughter, which seemed to belong to a person who was out of her mind. Micky knew her weakness, but she didn't dare tell it to Tom. Could what she was feeling be considered rather a perversion? She wasn't too sure about it. She sometimes felt like telling Tom to spank her on her buttocks when he penetrated her, but she held back. She mimed a complete orgasm, although she really wanted to feel pain during those moments of intimate pleasure. It would have really meant a lot to her.

Next day, at dawn, the girls didn't go to school, and a warm sun was melting the icy snow. Dana hadn't got out of the house for a long time and thought that a walk would do her good. She put on thick clothes and she went to Nina's room. She had to clear her thoughts somehow. She hadn't wanted to see the girl since that evening, when she instinctively did some things she was ashamed of. She wanted to know; was shame just on the surface, a forced enclosure of her feelings or did she just want Nina's love deep down her soul? Maybe she would find out if they went for a walk together.

She had run into the little girl twice in the hall, but she avoided to look at her, even though the girl showed her most beautiful smile to her. It was better that way.

Dana went slowly to the little girls' room, opposite the hall. Her heart was beating mightily. She knocked at the door slowly. Stella came out and showed a crooked smile.

'Dana!', she said, astonished.

'Where is Nina?'

'Come in, come in, she's here. We were dancing.'

Nina was wearing a little red and white satin dress, which she was supposed to wear on Christmas. She was also wearing some white flats.

'Is Christmas here?', laughed Dana shyly.

Nina stopped dancing, when she saw her protectress.

She was breathing discontonuously. Her eyes were shining. Dana had come to her. She had been upset for several days, had been crying, because the woman whom she loved the most in this world, had turned her back on her. What could she have possibly done wrong?

Dana came closer to her and took her hand.

'Are you ready for a walk?'

Nina hugged her tight, which meant that she was more than thrilled. She seemed to miss the time spent with Dana, when she could have given her the moon in the sky.

'Then, go get dressed.'

In less than 15 minutes, Dana and Nina were out of the orphanage, in one of the nearby roads.

'Why did you treat me like that?', asked Nina, holding the young woman's arm tight. 'Have I done something wrong? I wouldn't want to upset you for anything in the world.'

Dana thought whether a child could understand (even if she were 13, Nina was a child) what had happened then in her mind and soul. Her feelings jumbled over each other, as if wanting to make her dizzy. Who knows, maybe there were gaps, anxieties, even now, but at the moment, she wasn't brave enough to realise she had them.

She answered Nina that she didn't have to worry about anybody or anything else. Her little head had to remain immaculate, like a sheet of white paper. She had had some health problems, some not too pleasant moods which made her disagreeable. That was all.

'How could I not worry?', asked Nina. 'You are my mommy.'

They hugged.

'My mommy', she repeated, whispering with her eyes closed.

'Wretched mommy, who was caressing her child in a really strange way', thought Dana.

She was really glad that in Nina's mind she represented the mother the little girl had lost in prison.

God, it was such a relief that she hadn't given too much thought to what had happened. Was that how Nina realised everything? Maybe it had been a game for her.

'A terrible game'. It felt like losing one's mind.

In the evening, after a while (after having a warm cheeseburger and some milk with Nina and giggling at a puppet's show), Dana understood that she was not a pedophile, but she had a certain restraint when she thought about being a lesbian.

Did she like women? Did she like women in a certain way? Oh, how much did she want to forget that terrible evening, but she couldn't.

How could she not realise how she really felt? She could be bisexual, but no, she will not use Nina for her pervert games.

Was she afraid to admit that she was bisexual? She didn't know very well. But one thing was for sure. To Nina, it couldn't be but mother or sister love. And that vertiginous outburst that evening had been... she needed somebody to maintain her madness, to quench the fire in her body. And it didn't matter too much if it were a man or a woman. Or even a child? What a fool! She had been seeing Nina as a woman for a year now, a possible victim of her perversion. And God, no, she didn't want that. Now, all of a sudden, everything seemed less grey. Nina won't always be a child she'll always protect. Then, all the time, in fact during the year, she had chosen Nina because she was beautiful. The others were ugly and slatternly.

She didn't want Nina as her partner. You can be carried away by the wind to nowhere, and if you don't want to fall, he won't swallow you.

Dana won't be swallowed. She'll find other men and women as partners and no way will they be aurolacs from the market or the corner of the street. She wanted something good and refined. She'll know how to choose them, she was absolutely sure about that.

What else could she hope for her life? Not too many good things were waiting for her. If she doesn't get hired somewhere, she'll be thrown out in the street. If she couldn't work, it would be way over her head. She just wanted to be a BOSS. Like now. It was good. Well, but how about her sick mind? In the darkness there were lights, too. She actually knew how to part light from darkness, but she liked the wolf in a lamb's fur, in fact.

They finally returned to the orphanage, full of energy, although they had been walking all day long.

Dana had a calm night for the first time after a while, an undisturbed sleep, without any kind of dreams.

It was crystal clear. She wasn't a miserable pedophile, and giving it a deep thought, it wasn't even Nina whom she actually wanted. She had wanted for such a long time a woman whom she could touch intimately. Or, maybe a man. Dana didn't have fleeting relatioships, nor steady ones either. Her first man, a boy actually, was 19, and she was 14. He deflowered her on a hot July night in the girls' restroom. It was in a mixed dorm, somewhere at the border of the country. It smelled stridently of urine and blood. Her blood which was dripping on her skinny legs.

It had hurt her a lot and she cursed the boy for a while. After that, she had sex a couple of times, and then she gave up. She didn't feel much pleasure, and she sometimes hated men because, by their way of being, they were asses.

When she met Mario, the Italian, something moved deep in her soul. Mario was pretty different than the men she had met before. Mario was gentle, kind and warm-hearted. She once asked herself if behind that face there could hide something dirty, but she removed the thought quickly as if stepping on an insect. No. Mario represented everything that was good about men. She had lost him and had suffered a lot when he kissed her on her cheeks. 'I'll come and see you one day', he said smiling, and she cried, clinging on to him.

'I'll take you in Italy.'

Italy. Yeah, right. Still, one thing was important. He didn't forget her, sending postcards and photos. For a year, something had vibrated inside her and had had strange sensations but she could not make out too much what those feelings were, which sometimes frightened her.

The day she made up her mind to see Nina naked and caress her like a woman, her thoughts rustled in her head, tiring her. Did she or did she not want the the little girl?

This jumble of feelings made her suffer, but now she was happy because she knew some vices of hers, the real darkness in her soul.

Ms. Boobs started begging again. She gained enough

to buy a pizza for Dana and her. Sometimes, Micky came for a treat.

The snow had melted, even the asphalt had dried, so Bibi could walk freely. Dana also sent her this time after some money. She smiled dumbly. And she could never refuse Dana; because she was afraid to or just because, out of a certain fellow feeling.

Bibi shook the dirty training suit's pocket and realised she had scooped in quite a lot, and it wasn't even midday yet. She was glad, for Dana and her.

'What the hell are you doing?' she said, and her eyes widened with horror. It was him. Joe the madman, Joe the merciless, Joe the evil. Seeing her, he made faces, and his eyes shrank until they looked like cracks. She represented his enemy, but he had to hide the not so pleasant feeling that he was experiencing.

His lips curved in a dumb smile.

'What are you doing here?' His jeans and jacket were dirty, just like his niece's.

'Err... what are you doing?', stuttered Ms. Boobs. She hesitated to give him an answer. That man shouldn't ask her anything. To her, he represented a scum who wanted to take her house away from her.

'Listen', he said trying to sound humane, 'would you like to go out for coffee?'

Bibi pretended not to hear him and was about to leave, when he grabbed her sleeve.

'Don't you want to make peace with me?'

She grinned, exposing her ugly teeth.

'I'm not giving you the house', she said insipidly.

'Sure, sure.' The man became nervous. He had grabbed her arm more tightly.

'Don't make me become aggressive here in the street', he whispered, spitting the words through his teeth.

Bibi, in her ignorance, realised that Joe could sometimes be really repugnant.

'What do you want?'

'I want to tell you that you are stupid. Don't mess with me, or else, you'll lose'. Bibi glanced somewhere else, opposite the street. In the trouble she was in, the girl saw the little light of hope. It was far away, but she saw it. She'll tell Dana, and she'll know what to do.

'OK', she said conciliatorily. 'Let go of my arm'.

Joe let go of her arm satisfied. He pursed his lips and nodded his head as 'yes, you're a good girl, who does exactly what I tell her to do.'

'You want the house, don't you?'

'Stop asking stupid questions. That's life', said Joe smiling and looked up, then, with the nicotine stained finger, he sketched a circle in the air, a carousel. 'You get out, and I'll get in.'

'Ah, yes, yes', laughed Bibi, restraining her anger. 'Come tomorrow to the orphanage and we'll talk more'.

"I'll feel safer there."

'Hey, the world hasn't crashed down', said Dana to Ms. Boobs who was crying so hard that the walls were shaking.

Bibi told Dana everything, about her parents, about the house, and about Joe. About Joe, right from scratch. Joe, the madman.

Dana seemed amazed that her 'servant' herself owned a house, and she didn't. But she couldn't be envious of Ms. Boobs. It would have been too much.

'I'll be homeless', sighed Ms. Boobs. 'Help me, please.'

"So will I", thought Dana, and then said with a lost look:

'I'll help you, Bibi, I'll help you. Aren't I always your safety pillar?'

Did Bibi really understand this?

Bibi did understand it mostly, she loved and hated Dana. They were two flexible feelings. She could rely on her in difficult moments (like the one now) and would have spit her when she pretended to be the great princess, making her the humble and pathetic servant at the same time.

'Listen to me', complained Bibi, 'you have to help me'.

'Sure', said Dana calmly. 'Everything has a limit in this world. Everything.'

One day Joe came to the orphanage. A wonderful sun was heating the earth and winter was almost over.

Ms. Boobs had taken care to tell the guard (when seeing Joe) that he is her uncle and that he wanted to take him upstairs. The guard agreed.

On that day Dana was calm. Her forehead was serene, and her eyes, black as coal, were peaceful.

She was standing in the hall, stuck to the radiator, with her long hair tight in a ponytail. She was wearing a green training suit with the same incredibly white trainers. When Joe saw her, a hesitating smile flashed his body.

'A pretty little doll', he thought.

'A scoundrel with pig-like eyes", thought Dana.

Their thoughts didn't converge in any way in the same

direction. Bibi introduced them to one another, and Joe pretended to be a great gentleman, kissing Dana's hand (who shook with disgust), looking straight into her eyes.

They exchanged a few words such as 'What a nice lady, what do you do, you are paying a visit, aren't you?' Joe felt at ease, and he forgot about his niece, who left them alone. Then, Joe felt wonderful, when Dana asked him calmly and without too many detours.

'Do you happen to know a hotel somewhere?'

The man was desperately searching his pockets, his eyes were out of their sockets, and a greedy laughter contorted his face. There was always money for something like this.

A crazy game driven at the same time by a sexual passion and a plausible revenge (can revenge also be plausible?). Dana knew what the man wanted and that was what he would get. Joe woke up tied to the bed (just like he saw in films) by his arms and feet.

'Hey, this girl is wonderful, she must be wonderful.'

Dana made him undress, wearing only his dirty white underwear. It was better this way. Joe was miserable and she didn't want to see more. His clotted hair, under his arm, on his chest and legs was enough. But the most disgusting was the one coming out in tufts on the margin of his underwear.

But she had to do it. For her Ms. Boobs. Just as she was like, Bibi endured all her negative expression. Just like a faithful puppy, sometimes with tears in her eyes. Bibi waited for Dana to calm down, when she had nervous outbursts. Then, the "boss" hurt her. She hit her and held her closed in the room. She simply enslaved her.

Dana was sometimes really bad, but other times she just entered your soul like a light, warming it up. Just like now, for example.

Joe was drooling. He knew it would be a hell of a catch, and Dana was a beautiful girl.

'Don't be stupid', he said to himself, 'don't miss this opportunity.'

Dana was sure of her strength. The ties were very tight. The man was completely immobilised. Now the young woman stood still in the middle of the room, looking at him:

'You, miserable scum, heartless, pervert man.'

'Hey, what are you doing?' laughed Joe. 'Aren't we playing?'

Dana seemed calm but there was fire smoldering inside her. She bit her lower lip.

'What do you want?'

'Come on, come on, what can I say?' giggled Joe, 'you like playing tough. Maybe you want to look tough, but come on, Joe's cock can't wait anymore.'

Dana's lips became thinner and thinner until they looked like a stripe, then she said:

'We're living in a crazy world, aren't we?'

'Yeah, yeah, but come on over quicker, kitty', babbled Joe.

'Quickly. Where quickly? To the wilderness maybe, or to hell. Isn't it pretty much the same thing?'

The man was looking at her with protruding eyes.

'Come', he whispered.

The little bitch was playing with him, but he didn't always like games. And this was a pervert game. But he was getting impatient. He had been sweating.

Dana, still standing, said in a soft voice.

'The world will not disappear if you suffer.' She shut up a little, for a few seconds, and then kept on talking.

'You deserve to suffer.'

'Kitty!' Joe somewhat smelled something fishy. He started shaking his hands, but Dana had taken good care of it.

''You deserve to suffer', repeated the young woman. 'You don't have the right to threaten your own niece. Do you think that's fair?'

Joe spat.

'Bitch! Nobody does this to Joe!'

The girl burst into laughter.

'Ha, ha, ha, loser.' Suddenly, and then her voice became rough and tough. She got close threateningly to Joe, who was looking at her as if he were out of his mind.

'Brainless madman, see, the sun hasn't set for us yet, "the ones who do not belong to anybody". We are united, even if there are sometimes conflicts between us. You will leave Bibi alone, she is with me. I am her mistress and her protectress.'

'Bitch!'

'Hmmm', snorted Dana, 'madman, birdshit, you can die next to a ditch anytime. I have many "acquaintances in this area". Gypsies who will stab you with a knife in the back, without you knowing where it came from. Life's paths are really tangled.'

Joe was as white as a sheet.

'Get out', he screamed. 'You, miserable! And untie me.'

'Yes, I'll get out, but you'll do it right.' A smile widened on Dana's face.

'Nobody mocks at me. Nor at poor Bibi.'

Bibi knew very well why Dana had left with Joe. To punish him. An amazing joy invaded her. Nobody, ever since her parents died, had defended her. It was great. Dana was great. Dana was bad and great. She had that badness which would have made (if she could) her, Bianca Manole, slap her really hard over her insolent face so that blood came out of her nose, lips and broken eyebrow arch.

Then, she would have laughed like crazy (and it wasn't long until she got like that). What strange thoughts were crossing her mind, damned strange thoughts. She could have never hit Dana, and she didn't want to, but her punishment would have been much bigger and there was no point in it. She limited herself to listen to Dana, without transgressing her duties.

Bibi looked outside the window in her room. Darkness had fallen like a molasses surrounding everything. Only the street lights sprang, seeming phosphorescent.

She was lying in bed, with her knees to her chest, thinking about Dana and Joe. She was really curious about what had happened. Dana had always had her punishment methods. She had known how to impose herself and Bibi was sure she would put him in place as well. Joe the miserable.

A little later, Dana came. She entered the room, took off her coat and put it on one of the bunk beds.

She was smiling strangely, her lips seemed to be contorting, it was actually a grin, from which Bibi didn't understand anything. Was it black or white?

When she started talking, Dana was very convinced. Her voice seemed a little hoarse.

'Your uncle won't be disturbing you.'

She jumped in bed, put her hands under her head, and

she glanced up. A weak smile flourished on her lips. She was enjoying her victory.

Spring passed, like an explosion of fragrance and colour, and summer came. June days, warm and full of pleasure.

The girls kept on fighting hard for survival. They kept on fighting, scratching their fingernails, leaving blood trails, which were dripping on their skin. They didn't like anything. They didn't like food, nor the clothes they were given, not even the country where they were born, Romania.

'This country sucks!', Bibi shouted once, hitting the bed hard with her fist.

'You have nothing, you see nothing far away, just... poverty.'

Dana got two letters from Mario. They were in Italian, so she asked Maria, the nurse to tell her what her far away friend wrote to her (Maria had studied Italian in school).

Mario sent her greetings and apologised for not keeping in touch with her for so long.

'Damn', mumbled Dana, 'he had forgotten about her, and now, all of a sudden, he felt guilty.' Anyway, she was glad to see a photo with him, on the motorbike, with his long hair in the wind. How long had his hair grown!

Dana kissed the photo and her eyes moistened.

There were questions in her mind again, questions she hadn't been asking herself for quite a while. Did she like women or men? Was she bisexual? Possibly.

And also for a while, since spring came, she hadn't had strange thoughts and depressive states which caught her in a dense pitch darkness. She was happy she could feel life, exploit Ms. Boobs, make her beg for her, feel the centre of the universe, the mistress of the girls with behavioural disorders.

She went for a walk with Nina (obviously, as she was her favourite) and she never forgot to take sweets and refreshments. She was Nina's "mother", all loving and all knowing. Dana knew what was best for Nina. She even taught her how to use tampons during her period. Nina thanked her for everything and kissed Dana's both cheeks softly. Never will she find a person who will love her so much, give her even a small piece of her soul. And in her turn, she would give her all her heart and all the gentleness of her childhood.

They were two soulmates which attracted each other like magnets. Nina was the only person whom Dana gave love through the gate of her soul. For the rest, she kept some badness, humility and a little mercy, which was kept for Ms. Boobs. She knew how to enslave her, humiliate her, but she had something special, which urged her to protect her sometimes. Just like she did with Joe the madman, Joe the merciless. She had revenged Bibi.

Dana had many things, many distinct feelings, her own suffering, which drove her crazy, or on the contrary, emptied her thoughts, becoming a person for whom life and death were completely alike.

Dana was a complex character.

'Can you confront the world on your own?', Micky was thinking on the first summer day. If you are strong enough, maybe yes. She was sitting on a bench near Michael the Brave's statue. Her eyes were swimming in tears. Was it appropriate to cry for someone who wasn't worth it? If she loved him, he had meant for her the centre of her universe, the axle on which she propped her life.

A few days before, it had been Tom. She needed him, she wanted to feel loved in those moments. The sunset left long traces above the city when Micky arrived at his home.

She had found him bathed in perspiration with a bitch in his bed.

What did suffering mean, what is comfort, what is love, what is joy or maybe happiness? She had felt all these, and at the moment she was feeling deep pain.

Tom sat upright, looked at her with blurred eyes, and just babbled 'Micky'.

Had he been stunned to see her or was he thinking to see whether he recalled her name? How ridiculous! Wasn't he who had promised her forever love and lots of children? Micky left that 'stinking room' and walked astound in the street. Life was playing her a nice trick again. She never wanted to see him again and she was sure that, after his look, he was going to do the same. He hadn't loved her, he had just used her (who knows, she might have used him herself as well).

People were passing by into a dizzying to and fro, and she was looking at them holding her head in the back of her palm.

'Were they happy? Did they have everything that she didn't? Sure, they have thoughts, feelings, fears, depressions, joys, and sorrows.'

Then why did she feel marginalised? 'You come from an orphanage', screamed a stray thought. Micky slowly shook her head. No, that wasn't the reason. 'She was a gypsy', screamed another thought. 'It was ridiculous, we are all people who undoubtedly have the right to life.'

No, she really felt marginalised by her own way of thiking. The universe doesn't collapse, bu her support point has snapped. What does it mean to be happy or better said, can you live in a hut and be happy?'

The answer came from deep within her. YES. She had been happy, without any money, only with love. She had fed herself with love and hope. But doesn't hope die last? The lifeblood within us drips only when there is no hope left. Then the wings break and what is next? The fall.

Happiness consists of your own way of thinking. The more bitter you are on life, the deeper you immerse yourself in mud, black clouds hover above you and you don't foresee the disaster. A healthy way of thinking and a soul in communion with God will see the LIGHT.

What light? LIGHT = HAPPINESS.

Tears were falling on Micky's cheeks. They had come off later on from her eyes and were slipping on her dark skin.

Some of her suffering seemed to have melted like snowflakes on hot asphalt. The tears seemed to be washing the sorrow of the soul.

Micky sat on the bench, without being hungry or thirsty, until the lights of the city turned on. Then she slowly went to the orphanage.

There sometimes passed seconds, minutes, hours, days one after the other without something good happening. The girls would fight, pull out their hair and take anybody or anything into account. An avalanche of follies, which linked one after the other, day after day.

Dana laughed from ear to ear, when everything became

muddy, when fights became tougher, and when the grey enveloped the orphanage. What could she say, everything was crazy, a game of madmen (or better said, of mad women) in a madhouse. And she was the initiator, she gave the tone.

The headmistress tried to talk to the 'young ladies', as she called them, but she didn't reach any result. The girls would hum her, and as ever, madness prevailed in the orphanage. Two psychologists had also been called, who had tried talking to Bibi, who seemed to have gone mad (and that with Dana's consent), Micky and Stella, the girl who wanted to become a boy.

'You'll never become a boy if you hit your colleagues', one of the psychologists said to Stella.

The girl was sitting on a plush armchair, legs crossed. A sly smile appeared on her lips, and she closed her eyes for a few seconds, and then she suddenly opened them as if a stray and important thought dawned on her.

'What are you saying? Aren't I going to be a boy? You are one ugly liar', she said to the red-haired woman, older than 50. 'You know very well that it can't be.'

How had she come to this conclusion?

One morning, two months ago, Dana, very bored, totally depressed, saw her in the hall, and called her.

'Stella, do you still want to be a boy?' (everybody had found out about the girl's wish).

Stella giggled, then widened her eyes as if she had seen a priceless treasure.

'Can you do something, Dana?' Then she hummed as if she were an accomplice.

Dana put an arm on the girl's shoulders.

'Baby, would you just listen to me, please?'

'Yes, Dana.'

Dana shut up for a few moments, which seemed an eternity to Stella. Dana couldn't help her or what? Dana went on, moistening her lips with her tongue.

'Everything is a lie, Stella. Everyone is lying to you. You will never be a boy.'

Stella's eyes filled with tears. She wanted to say something, but Dana put a finger on her lips, whispering.

'Everything is a lie. Everything is a LIE.'

Stella suffered after a while after she talked to Dana, there, blankly, but realised that what the young woman had said to her was true. Why? Because Dana always told the truth. 'Try doing whatever you want.'

She wanted to be bad and aggressive. She wanted to be like Dana, so that the girls would be afraid of her. And she would maintain order among the little girls who wouldn't obey. She would be a real 'man'. Didn't she always want that?

The lady psychologist took a deep breath.

'Yes', she said conciliatorily, 'you may be right, I may have lied to you, but that was so that you wouldn't suffer.'

'Damn it! You wanted to annihilate my energy, and if you had done that, I wouldn't be like Dana. I won't be a leader. Do you understand? And leave me alone', screamed Stella and got out, slamming the door behind her.

Bibi and Micky also talked ugly with the other psychologist.

'You don't know and you will never know anything, you don't know what it is like to spend your life in orphanages', said Bibi angrily. 'Err... you don't know anything', she mumbled.

'People cheat on you everywhere', Micky gasped and cursed Tom in mind.

The grey-haired headmistress had to do something. She couldn't let chaos prevail, throwing around with restlessness and disagreement. She hadn't done anything with the psychologists. The women hadn't been able to bring tranquility and calm in the souls of the girls with behavioural disorders. What was there to be done?

After a while, it was concluded that they had to talk to Dana. Why? Simply because the girl coordinated everything. If a war started, then this war started with Dana's approval, if there had to be peace, Dana raised the white flag. One day, Maria, the nurse, called the young woman to her medical office (the grey-haired headmistress had suggested that, taking into account the fact that the nurse 'was getting along well' with Dana, at least she thought so).

The girl entered the medical office, with her hands thrust in her white capris. She was clean and tidy as usual. Maria invited her to sit down, trying to address her a weak smile.

'You told me that you wanted to talk', said Dana. 'What is it?'

Maria pulled a chair and sat in front of the young woman.

'Does it have to be something? Can't we discuss, just like that? You look for me only when you need me. Now I need you.'

'Hm', snorted Dana... 'I don't know.'

She only knew that Maria had helped her in her moments of bitter depression, crueller than death.

'Do you want to help me?'

Maria had never needed her help, the help of an unbalanced person. Why was she doing it just now?

'Listen to me', startd Maria. 'Do you see how the sun is shining in the sky? One day, maybe you'll shine like that. And that is if you listen to me.'

'Nonsense. Is this woman rambling?'

'It seems to you that I am talking nonsense, doesn't it?', said Maria, as if reading her thoughts.

There's a lot of misery in this world, why do we have to dirty it as well? I mean, you can do a lot for your part of the world we live in.

"That must be a an emotional blackmail." She couldn't ask her everything, she couldn't kidnap her perversion, which pulled her out of the dark shadows.

'What are you asking from me?', asked Dana, trying to look calm.

'Make this masquerade stop, this war broken out between the girls.'

Dana grinned. Now she had to defend herself.

'There has always been war. They are sick. "Just as sick as you", whispered a thought of hers.

Maria took a deep breath, then exhaled slowly. It was difficult to fight with Dana. It was better to have her as an ally than as an enemy. She was like a fish. When you thought you caught it, it slipped quickly through your fingers. Just like that.

'You know very well what I am talking about', said Maria. 'You are their leader, isn't it enough?'

"Emotional blackmail. You helped me, shouldn't I do the same?"

Why did Maria need gratitude? She thought she was different.

'You want me to stop the war, don't you?'

'Yes, I do.'

Who wants that, the old grey-haired woman or those stupid lady psychologists, who don't even know what world they live in? I thought you would become my friend shortly. But you are a hyprocrite', groaned Maria.

Maria couldn't retreat and didn't want the girl to make a wrong impression about her.

'I want everything to be fine, I want tranquility and a lot of pleasure to work with you. In these conditions, my heart is broken, And I want to be your friend, I am your friend.'

'No, you're nor my friend', Dana got out slamming the door.

"They wanted to kidnap those dirty games, which distracted her attention from her own helplessness."

Maria remained lost in thought. As the headmistress said. She was the young girl's only escape. Dana had refused her last chance. Maria's eyes were full of tears. Will she hate her for her future? And she'll never stand her look when she meets her.

Maria was thinking. She had never known how to talk, she could never reveal her true feelings and make them communicate with Dana's feelings. Tears were falling, washing her cheeks. The world was indeed a carousel of follies.

Dana had suffered a lot, was it the case for her to suffer even more?

However, she did evil, she dug it from its roots so that it would grow. She liked seeing how it grew, even though her soul was bitter. Maria definitely knew that.

Almost all the personnel of the centre didn't want Dana anymore. She should have gone somewhere she actually belonged. And all knew what the solution was – the hospital hospice.

'Maybe for a while', said the headmistress. 'She'll know how to respect her peers and she'll learn that life is not just a game, a carousel where you you spin until you get dizzy. She'll learn not to cause harm.'

"Or she'll end up in a madhouse", thought Maria. It was painful to even think about the hospice-hospital. The girl had once gone there to see what it was like and she thought only about it for some time. It was a true valley of grievance.

When the headmistress proposed this solution, and all the others accepted it, Maria felt revolt.

'However, it may be too drastic a measure, madam manager. It'll deepen in...'

"Darkness", she would have wanted to say. "Lots of darkness, blackness, which will probably put her to eternal sleep".

The headmistress's look was rough.

'She needs a lesson.'

Dana had had several lessons, Maria knew that too well, lessons which she may have applied on her own or life itself had applied them. Dana caused problems, brought out an air of superiority, but she was in fact weak. She wanted to hide her weakness, throwing in others with malice and aggression.

Maria had nothing to do. She had to comply with the plan. Dana would go to a world emptied of love. Would she be able to endure that? Here, Nina, the pretty girl, loved her very much. And Maria cared for her a lot. There, everybody would consider her an intruder, who had to be punished.

There were two women and a man. The women seemed young, but the man was older and had a moustache.

They entered the headmistress's office, stayed there for more than half an hour, then got out accompanied by her, smiling and talking continuously.

Maria was on duty that day. She was just giving pills to some girls. She got out for a moment and saw them. Her heart started beating a little faster. Had they come for Dana?

It was morning, the sun had already risen in the sky and it looked like it was going to be a warm day.

The headmistress saw the girl and called her.

'We might need you. The gentlemen came to pick Dana up.'

The girl's soul startled. It was exactly as she had expected. The fight was about to begin.

'Are you sure?', the girl babbled.

One last chance would a truly wonderful thing. A sad smile bloomed on her lips, hoping, at the same time.

The headmistress frowned her eyebrows and she seemed uglier than ever to Maria.

'What's up with you? This girl really deserves a lesson.

Don't try to convince me, because you won't succeed. She has to know what "keeping calm" means.'

Maria moistened her lips, looking in turn at the women and the old man in front of her.

'Do you think that she'll learn there?'

'Maybe.' And the headmistress turned around.

They made an attempt which could destroy a person. Attempts, these will be waiting for Dana, and she'll have to hang in there. But, knowing her weakness, Maria doubted it. She'd disappear completely through darkness or she would see the light, which was quite unlikely. Only God knew.

Dana hadn't opposed when the headmistress with a high-pitched voice told her that she would leave the hospice for a while. "You'll learn to appreciate what you have", said the woamn. The girl didn't do anything but spit on the carpet and kicked. There was Bibi, Ms. Boobs there (who otherwise was glad that she would remain the boss there), Micky, the gypsy, and Stella, the boy-girl.

Micky was a little sad, and so was Stella. They would't have a person to lead them. Stella thought that Dana had told her that she would never become a boy, and thus, those bitches had lied to her. Dana had done her a favour, now who was going going to help her anymore? Dana put her clothes in a big plastic bag and when ready, she looked at her colleagues without starling at all. Her face was almost immutable, just like a statue. Then, she looked at Maria and said, insensibly:

'I want to see Nina.'

The girl was sleeping when Dana kissed her on her

cheek. She woke up, and when she saw her, a large smile brightened her face. The young woman took her in her arms and held her tight to her chest.

'I want you to be good and love me, at least a little, I must know that there is an ounce of love for me in your heart.'

Nina cried a lot after Dana had left. Now she was alone, and the "vipers" would pounce on her.

She had nights when the dreamed repetead compulsively. She was with Dana holding hands in a green meadow with lots of flowers, laughing joyfully, eating her favourite chocolate biscuits, then a strong wind, like a dust cloud, took Dana, lifted her in the sky, and knocked down, dead. And Nina would cry out loud next to the lifelessbody. She would wake up bathed in sweat, and her heart would beat almost breaking her chest. And mom wasn't by her side. She was far, far away. She would get into trouble, because that was what it was like at the centre, and she didn't have anybody to tell it to, nobody listened to her. Her suffering might truly start from now on.

It was late at night, and Dana couldn't sleep. She looked at the stars through the barred windows (she didn't have bars at the centre). It was Hell on Earth there. She had come for a few hours, and time was passing harder than eternity.

She had been put in a dirty white room with shriveled and damp walls, here and there.

A stray flashed through her mind. "I'm going to die here, in this stinking bed, which smells like shit, I'll probably die tonight. There are lots of stars, and I'm going to be one of them.'

There were two other girls in the room; Vera was 26 years old, and she was autistic (she lived in her own world), and Claudia, 24, limp, very deformed legs, but she was brainy. When Dana was brought into the room, she got up very slowly and she exposed her decayed teeth in a crooked smile.

'One more has come', she said.

Good, thiught Dana, at least this one was taliking, because the other one came towards her and hit her in the shoulder. Dana pushed her spitefully and hissed a curse through her teeth. The educator accompanying her showed her the bed, and then got out babbling "I hope you'll get along well."

Certainly, everything will be much better than the fairytales with Prince Charming. Dana closed her eyes for a few seconds. It smelled like disease, madness, rot there. She wouldn't be able to survive there.

She refused dinner, because she felt like throwing up. The hall was full of young people with issues, who crawled at the margin of society, and didn't seem to affected by that. They were disabled.

Maybe Ms. Boobs was disabled, but not like that. The hospice could very well be considered a madhouse.

Dana saw herself alone, in a world where normal people forgot her. She was stuck to a thick concrete wall, and her frail body felt the coldness acutely. Her domineering feeling was melting little by little, but she knew herself too well, and she knew it would appear again anytime.

A strange noise could be heard, and in the darkness of

the room, where only the street light flickered, Dana saw how Vera tore her pyjama in her sleep.

The young woman turned her head. 'God', she whispered.

Now she fiercely wanted to sleep. She tried thinking about something nice, but it was also dark in her mind. 'Darkness and suffering everywhere.'

Nina's cute face suddenly appeared before her eyes. She had a crooked smile in the corner of her mouth, and her big eyes seemed to shine.

Dana smiled for the very first time since came to the hospice. With eyes closed, she would call Nina and beg her to call her "mom".

Then she saw Mario on the motorbike, dressed in leather, with his face as white as a sheet. He was handsome, just like he was in the photos he had sent to her, and which the girl took with her.

She fell asleep thinking about Mario and Nina and she didn't hear anymore how Vera fell off the bed.

'Hm, hm, hm', she said, and then she made some imperceptible sounds, and got under the thin blanket again.

'How are you?' Claudia's grin was so ugly, that Dana was about to spit her right in the eye. It wasn't too pleasant to wake up in the morning seeing how someone seemed to laugh in your nose.

Dana sat upright.

'What do you want?'

Claudia was barely standing. She had short spiky hair,

and blue and incredibly small eyes (in fact, one was bigger than the other), and she spread a stale stench.

'How are you?', she repeated.

Dana stood up nervously, grabbed her arm, and almost dragged her to her bed.

'If you're crazy, you don't have to drive me crazy. I'll sit here, all right?', screamed Dana. She headed towards her bed, but turned her head and looked at Claudia.

'Don't you move from there!' She raised a finger towards her threateningly.

This time, Claudia started laughing slowly, then louder and louder, ha, ha, ha. Her eyes filled with tears.

'Look, look at you', she said, tearfully, 'you've got scared.'

A trail of saliva was dripping from her lips.

Dana suddenly got out of bed and hit her hard in the face.

'You, madwoman!' she said, being a bundle of nerves.

Claudia kept laughing, even though blood was dripping abundantly from her cracked lip.

Then Dana pulled out her spiky hair and knocked her down face up.

'Madwoman, madwoman, shut up!' Her strange laughter drove her crazy. Then Claudia stopped laughing, and put two fingers in her mouth. Dana saw her dumb look.

'Why am I bothering with you?', she said as if to herself. Her heart was beating strongly. She looked downwards, disarmed, and thought. 'What am I doing here? Why are these girls crazy? Why am I so aggressive? Whay do I like playing with people's lives? If I hadn't done it, I wouldn't have gotten here.' She looked at the two girls. 'Did they want to be here?'

'Did you want to be here?', she screamed.

Claudia was sucking her fingers vigorously, and Vera was smiling stupidly.

‚She's got a nice smile', thought Dana. 'If death hadn't existed, what would have happened? People would have lived for thousands and millions of years, would haven gotten tired of life, of suffering... I don't know what would have happened', thought Dana. Things would have been different, the entire universe would have been different. Would the stars have stayed differently in the sky?

Dana smiled bitterly. She was stupid for asking herself stupid questions. But in such a stupid place maybe it wasn't forbidden to ask yourself stupid questions.

Later on, a nurse came and called them for breakfast. Vera had wet herself and she changed her diapers.

'Move, idiot', she said, and shoved her. Then she addressed to Dana.

'You are new, aren't you?'

'Yes, the o-ring missing from the chain', said Dana bitterly (and thought whether the woman knew what an o-ring actually was.)

'I've heard that you're grounded. You see, everything is not pink at all. Behave properly so that you shouldn't get into trouble.'

'Yeah, right', said Dana.

It was the first time Dana had entered the dining hall. A large room, dyed in white, plastic tables, covered with a red and green cloth. But it was not that place which was desolating, it was the people sitting at the table. Young people above 18 years old each severe disabled. Dana looked at almost all of them closely and was sure that each of them had their story. A few girls and boys smiled at her, inviting her to take a seat next to them. Dana put on a little smile, which looked more of a grin. Then she suddenly turned around and headed towards the door.

'Hey, you, whereto?', said the fat red-haired cook.

In response, Dana scuttled.

Outside, the sun was shining in the sky which had no trace of clouds whatsoever. The girl burst into tears. In the yard surrounded by the grey concrete fence, Dana cried for a while. She couldn't know how long, for an hour, half an hour, she had lost track of time, and dashed into a sweet bitterness.

The tears seemed to wash the darkness in her soul, relaxing her body at the same time. Her shoulders were falling heavy, chilling off from the burden of sadness, burdens, detaching from them and falling in the deep imaginary fountain in front of them, all te suffering and the bitter moods melting like butter in the sun.

After a while, she sat on the concrete bench, which was the same colour as the fence.

She had wiped her tears, and for the first time after a long while, she inspired eagerly the warm air of the summer morning. It was good that the sun was shining in the sky and had sent her a little light. A shred, only a shred, but it had been enough.

The meal had probably finished. She wasn't hungry, but she heard her stomach squeaking, indignant.

Dana pressed her palm on her chest and heard her heart ticking, like a clock, regularly and quietly. She looked at the view in front of her.

The young people were wearing shabby clothing. Some

had eaten and their sweaters were spotted with oil and jam. A girl didn't seem to be older than 20, she was biting eagerly from a slice of bread, and she threw the ham on it on the asphalt.

Dana couldn't believe it. The centres where she had been, even since she was little, were true hotels. Here, everything was dismal and desolate.

The young people's faces, with slanting eyes and twisted mouths, made her believe that a horror film was on right in fron of her. Only the protagonists were real, so real that she shuddered.

She thought about Nina again and about the girl's gentleness. Then about Ms. Boobs, Micky and even strange Stella (who knows, maybe she wasn't that strange). They were her "servants" whom she was terribly missing now. They may have been her cornerstones. She enjoyed being an authoritative ruler, precisely because she was the least capable. Bibi was capable of begging (maybe she was a little foolish and she wasn't aware of the ridicule), Micky had been able to live with a man and always ready to take life by the throat, and Stella had so much faith that she would one day become a man (but now her wish had gone away).

Dana thought. She didn't have anything. Only malice. At least that was what she was thinking at the moment, when her mind was clear like a clear sky. She had been bad and she was sure she would be bad again. She couldn't change, just like that, all of a sudden, and she didn't want to. She wanted to be strong, even though she felt it wasn't like that.

The girl with the bread came closer. She smelt strongly

of sweat, and when she smiled, she didn't have the front teeth. She looked like a vampire.

She sat on the bench and went on smiling. She stopped chewing, and grinned this time. Her saliva was dripping from the corners of her mouth, disgracefully. She mumbled something and streched her hand with rugged fingers to Dana.

'Tete', she said, patting the young woman on the shoulder.

'OK', said Dana, making a grimace, 'and you are dumb. But it's such a pity that you aren't aware of that.'

She knew that she was bad, but she would never be able to understand these poor sufferers.

She got up from the bench (to the grief of the girl with the bread, who pursed her lips) and started walking slowly through the yard with her hands stuck in her shorts' pockets.

She saw Vera and Claudia, who were sitting on a bench. They smiled dumbly and waved at her. Then a few young people came to her.

'You're new, aren't you?', said a girl with a slight retardation.

'Yes', said Dana flatly.

They went on asking questions which bored Dana. Where does come from? How old are you? What is she doing here? Then a boy touched her hair gently, and Dana shuddered.

'He's handsome', he said with glowing eyes.

Another one said:

'And she is also beautiful.'

Dana left in a hurry. She was on the verge of crying again but she refrained, it was useless to do it anymore.

Anymore the show had begun. She had to play or withdraw. She'll think about that later.

She entered the hall and a pleasant coolness surrounded her. Her stomach revolted again and she headed towards the kitchen. The door was open and knocked strongly.

'Hey, is anyone here?' Nobody answered for a few seconds, then the fat red-haired cook came.

'What is it? What is it? You'll knock down the door.'

'I want to eat', said Dana roughly.

'Mealtime has just passed', the woman said and was about to close the door. Then Dana grabbed the doorknob.

'I'm hungry', she said, winking quickly. She was about to burst, if the woman hadn't whispered conciliatorily.

'Fine, fine, let me give you two sandwiches.' The young woman sighed. Through the transparent windows, she saw the sun shining. She was somewhat calmer now.

Bibi, Ms. Boobs, went on begging again. For a while, after Dana left, she had the feeling that the world was hers, she turned into the most glowing girl of the centre. She was her own boss, she didn't have such an authoritative boss, who had sometimes grinded her life. Would she know how to impose herself, just like Dana had done? What, wasn't she able to do it? She thought about it for a few seconds, then she didn't find the answer, and had to admit – Dana knew how to impose herself. But what had she done with that? She'd rot in a strange place, with people just as strange. How did she know? She had heard the nurses talk.

'It's Hell on Earth there', said one of them.

'The sun always sets there', said another one.

And a few days after Dana leaving, she heard some bad things.

'She deserved to go there.'

'Nobody could do her anything here.'

'She'll know what respect is.'

Bibi had always been afraid of Dana. If she didn't something welll, Dana knew how to impose herself. Beating was no longer a secret. Dana sometimes used to beat her colleagues, when they didn't obey. Bibi sometimes hated her for that, but she indulged in many not so pleasant things, which Dana instructed her to do. For instance, begging. And Ms. Boobs enjoyed begging, and was really happy when Dana gave her a smile of hers as a sign of appreciation, 'yes, my obedient puppy, I think you deserve a little bone.' And gave her a big slice of pizza with mushrooms and lots of sauce, then coke. Bibi was happy those moments.

Now she was standing in the street and thinking. If at first she was happy that Dana had left, now, after more than two weeks, it seemed that she was missing her. Maybe Dana was her safety pole, she had given her life and tranquility. Strange, but at the moment, that was what she was thinking.

She didn't have anyone to share food with, and she didn't have any reward for the work she had done. There wasn't that smile anymore, which Dana used to wave, like a flag. It wasn't Dana anymore. Her eyes suddenly filled with tears and a feeling of sadness surrounded her. She looked through her hanoracks's large pockets. She had gathered lots of money, so she wouldn't beg anymore. She would settle for a cup of coffee and a croissant tonight. She didn't want more. She headed towards the centre, and a stray thought suddenly flashed through her mind. How nice it would have been if

Dana had loved her as much as Nina had! Unbearable Nina! She had been Dana's favourite and she hadn't lifted one finger for that! She wanted to have everything for granted, that damned girl. Even feelings.

One morning, Nina came to ask Bibi if she knew anything about Dana.

'If you don't, I'm going to see her', she said proudly.

Her very arrogant attitude annoyed Ms. Boobs; even though she was a child, Nina knew she owned Dana's heart.

'If I don't want you to go, you won't go', groaned Bibi. A vein was visibly twitching at her neckline. 'Go! You think you're too smart and that's not OK.'

Nina called her 'a madwoman' and Bibi shuddered of nerves. Under the influence of the momentum, she hit her in the face so hard that blood came out of the broken lip. Then she pulled out her hair so savagely that she knocked her down.

'Madwoman, madwoman!' screamed Nina in pain. 'I'm going to tell you to Dana.'

'Get out!', screamed Bibi, full of hatred and maybe pain. The girl got out stumbling, and Bibi screamed after her.

'You think you are the centre of the universe, don't you?' She was breathing very hard, and she felt how malice was bursting from her lungs.

Damned girl, damned child. She would have given her beans. She would have gladly pulled out her her hair.

Bibi was walking in a street close to the centre. The sun was setting slowly above the city.

She stood like that a little, thinking for a while, then she went to the centre. She would send Stella to buy her the coffee and the croissant, although she was sure that the girl would like to share them with her.

Micky was biting heartily from the cheese sandwich and, from time to time, she was sipping the mint tea. It lacked sugar, but it was washing her throat. She looked at the clock, and put the entire slice into her mouth. She looked out of the window. It was rainin heavily during this end of July. But it was a warm rain and that was why she was wearing a short-sleeved blouse and a deep cleavage. She was very proud of her big elastic boobs.

She got out of the kitchen quickly, said a quick 'bye', she ran into the cook who called her 'crazy', and she rushed to school. She didn't miss Dana that much, although she behaved pretty well with her.

Maybe she needed a lesson. She had ventured too much in a story which she thought it was endless. But everything had an end. She thought she was their absolute boss, of the girls. 'God is our only master', thought Micky one evening. She had no right. She obeyed Dana, because she was sometimes afraid of her. Dana could sometimes become really aggressive. Micky was also aggressive, but she didn't go too far, a few fights in the centre, or in the street, just because she was challenged. After a difficult period in her life, her breakup with Tom, especially, she recovered and learnt how to walk on her road, even thouh there were brambles on both sides. She had learnt to pull them out. She wasn't after men anymore. Not all, but almost all only wanted one thing. She had given herself to one man with lots of love and the only thing she received was suffering.

Damn it with men. She'd work until she got something out of her life and she'd prove that she could give more then what she was asked.

It was still raining heavily and Micky got quickly wet on her hair and face. She looked up in the sky and smiled. She was really happy. One day, a while ago, she went to church, stood somewhere near the exit, looked at the icons and paintings on the wall, and had the felling that a blessed peace ot into her heart. The church was almost empty, there were about two or three women who didn't seem to notice her.

She was standing and didn't know what to say, because she didn't know any prayers. Finally, with a clear mind, she whispered, 'God, help Dana.'

The Virgin's face was glowing from the miracle working icon, and Micky looked at it intensely for a few seconds. It was wonderful. She had never seen such spelndour.

She got out with her heart as light as a snowflake. She had never been in a church before. Why now?

She was goin to buy hot bagels, when a woman asked her where 'The Assumption of Virgin Mary' church was. Nobody had asked about a church before, but then that women did. She knew about the church, it was somewhere near the street with the bagel shop. She went with the woman, she thought for about a second or two, and she entered. She had never talked to God, but maybe she didn't know how. She would learn how, though. She suddenly thought of something. Maybe Dana would learn how to talk to God one and for all because that was how she could be happy. She really wanted to pay Dana a visit, and she would talk to her about God and Virgin Mary, about lots of things. She wanted that the words would flow, and alleviate her suffering. And that was because she was sure that Dana was suffering. Dana didn't know how to be humble, maybe not even she, Micky, didn't know, they were two rebels, but the former was now tight as in a vice.

Micky was soaked when she got in the bus to go to school. She was 20 years old, but she would finish vocational school and work to support herself.

She'd have money, who knows, maybe she'd find someone who'd be compatible with (maybe men were not that bad).

She looked out of the window how it was raining, and she went on smiling.

Stella looked at the big window in the bathroom. She had her hair cut short, the curly hair was gone. She was wearing a white vest, the tender boobs were pushing the material, and training trousers.

'I'm a true Van Damme, I am handsome...' she was crooning slowly, arranging her haircut. 'I'm good-looking, and I'll become a boy one day.'

Aha, she did a karate number, and her eyes got a certain tension. She'd knock everybody down, she could fight with everybody. She alreay saw herself as the boss of the girls at the centre. For a second or two, she looked at herself in the mirror, let her arms slip heavy along her body, and said:

'I want to be like Dana.'

Dana meant for her a true boss, who had known how to lead. Sometimes, during the nights when she couldn't sleep, she used to think about Dana. She sometimes loved her (as much as she could care for someone), other times, she felt a strange envy and hate, which merged inside her and caused her a headache. Why was Dana the boss? It wasn't right. Maybe... maybe she had to be the boss. Then other thoughts surrounded her. What the hell was in her head? Bran or brain? How could she take decisions, control Ms. Boobs and even Micky? It was better to let herself controlled. Dana had behaved well with her. Stella hadn't realised though, that she had only been a tool for the young woman, to achieve certain goals. Dana sometimes revenges on the centre's management with Stella's help. The girl was easy going and easy to be led. She knew how to shape her, and when Dana said something, she was very credible (just like she did with the psychologist who lied to Stella that she was going to become a boy).

Stella went on looking at the window, taking different battle poses. She suddenly saddened a little. Dana had told her that she would never become a boy. Was that true? She remembered how much she had suffered when believing in Dana. Her words still resounded in her ears.

'Everyhting is a lie, Stella, everyboys' lying to you. You'll never become a boy.'

Stella had strongly pursed her lips and groaned nervously. Stella got nervous really quickly.

Crazy! Crazy Dana. She didn't know anything, she was nothing.

Nothing, nothing, NOTHING.

Two days ago, the gray-haired headmistress had solemnly promised that she would become a boy soon.

Stella believed her, maybe that was for the best. She had hope and that was wonderful.

She got out of the bathroom, threw away the towel with which she had wiped herself, and then ent down the stairs, almost hopping. It was a wonderful day, the sun had been up for a long time in the clear sky, and she would feel just as wonderful. To hell with Dana, she'd just have to rot there, in that cursed place.

'Hey', said Dana to Claudia, 'stick your fingers in your throat and take out the bread. You'll choke. Do you want to die?'

Claudia was sitting on the bed, with her head on one side, and she almost got bruised all over. She was snorting strangely and despite Dana's indifference towards 'the waste mob' (as she called the ones in the hospice), she got scared. She didn't want anybody to die. She hated death, she didn't understand this phenomenon too well, and she sometimes wanted to join it, and disappear for ever, saluting the world one last time, which was creaking from all joints.

'Take out the bread, damn you', screamed Dana. 'You really want to die, puny?' She lifted her with all her force from the bed and hit her soundly in the back. She didn't realise how strong she was. The crust came out, and Claudia breathed discontinuosly, having a terrible hunger for air.

'Dana, err... Dana...'

'Shut up', said Dana, 'stay calm now, stupid.'

She closed her eyes for a few moments and took a deep breath. She didn't want anybody to die. At the moment she hated cruel, cold death. At the moment she was wondering what death was? She thought that she had asked Mario, just like that, it suddenly came to her mind.

93

'Death is a gate', Mario told her, 'through which people enter, reaching other energetic levels.'

Hm, could it be nonsense? Was OK to die or not? Why are people so afraid of death?

"At one time it will tear all of us", thought Dana. Death a bag thin for sure. Bad, bad, bad. Dana frowned her eyebrows. She was nervous and she didn't know why. A bitter restlessness make her entire body tingle. At the moment she hated everybody. She felt closed like in a cage, and the key had been thrown away, who knows... maybe in the sea.

She started walking slowly in the room. She and she opened the window.

She looked at Claudia. She had told her with a squeaky voice in the morning:

'Dana, I've got my... period.'

That was it, it stank of blood, misery, just like it stank when Ms. Boobs had her period. Ms. Boobs didn't quite like water. She said that herself, whenever she was told to wash herself.

'I'm cold when I wash myself, even in the middle of a hot summer.'

Dana went on walkin in the room. At one point, she stopped and groaned towards Claudia.

'Why don't you wash yourself, girl? I feel how we're choking, do you hear me, even with the window open. Soon we'r going to bed, and I won't be able to breathe because of you. Do something for you and, of course, for me. You'd make a big charity. Claudia looked at her with incredible big eyes, and her face expressed a huge bewilderment.

'What is it?', said Dana to her. 'Isn't it OK what I'm saying?Am I wrong, dolly?' A grin appeared on her lips.

'Get up!', she screamed.

Claudia went on 'not understanding her.'

Dana didn't say anythin, grabbed her arm and dragged her to the bathroom near their room's door. The girl was walking too heavily, fell, babbled something, got up, and went forward.

'You, hobbling, stinky!', screamed Dana, full of nerves.

She had one of her nervous breakdowns.

'That's right, take off your clothes', she went on screaming. 'I'm not going to sleep with a trash next to me.

All of you are stinky, your period is stinky, this life is stinky.'

She turned off the cold water, lowered her head, and breathed heavily, as if after a long physical effort. She had a terrible headache. She ran quickly to the bathroom, feeling how her tears stung her eyes.

A day ended again and a day between the shrivelled walls of the hospital-hospice was really black. A repugnant world in which uncertainty was swarming so much. Everything was uncertain, how long were these young people going to stay here, actually, if they ever left, would one of them have a real chance to recover? It was unlikely that a special glow would light up their blurry minds. The night fully settled, the street lights were piercing the darkness and the room where Dana was staying was also swimming in darkness with a few rays of light glowing here and there.

The young woman had fallen asleep crying. Her soul was

heavy, two cannon balls were hanging on her shoulders, she could even see them with her mind's eye. They were damn heavy and the girl felt that she couldn't stand them anymore. Sometimes, like the moment she saw Claudia trembling under the gusts of cold water, she felt guilty because of the malice that was lying inside her. However, her instinct was too strong. Her tears seemed to wash this negative side of hers and she didn't think of anything anymore. She fell asleep.

It was past midnight when she woke up. She suddenly sat upright. She had been dreaming about snakes, lots of snakes, that were pulling out thin tongues at her, with protruding eyes, as if instigating her to alienation. She was running through the thicket (just like the one in her life), she was tripping over branches, falling and getting up. The snakes were really quick, they were arching in the air, curling and taking out macabre roars of laughter. How could they laugh and pull out those ugly tongues at the same time? The girl felt how her heart got out of her chest, she felt the heartbeats spasmodically in her throat. And the moment she woke up she felt her heart breaking her chest. She put a hand on it, hoping to calm it down. She was engulfed by a strange fear. She was a fool. What was she afraid of in fact? Of death! ... her thoughts screamed simultaneously. She started laughing slowly. Did she happen to love this stinky life? Could her inner self venture into having such feelings? Yes, she could love life or was she doing that out of pride? She sometimes thought she was strong and wanted to live to be a boss and especially show off her negative side. She will be BAD. She would hide the glimpse of kindness in her soul, her weakness (she knew very well that she could be very weak). Here, in Hell, she won't show it to anybody, and that is because nobody deserves this.

Her heartbeats calmed down a little. Now she was calm and her fear disappeared. She felt better. She lay again. It was warm and she threw the pillow on the ground. Then she heard the door, and the nurse who was on the night shift came in.

'What's happening here?' she said. 'Go to sleep!' She smoked from the lit cigarette.

'And you put off the cigarette, I'll tell you to the manager', said Dana calmly.

'Oh, really, do you dare talk again?'

'No, Vera.'

The woman turned on the light and neared Dana. She was fat and smelt of sweat. She threw the cigarette out of the window.

'I know you are here for good behaviour, and I know it's hard for you among lunatics, but what can I do for you? If you had had an ounce of brain, you would have minded your own business.'

'Yes', said Dana cynically. 'You are so right!'

'I sure am.' The woman seemed thrilled. 'Go to sleep.'

Dana turned her back at her.

'Go and wash yourself. You stink terribly.' Then se suddenly got up. Her lips turned thinner into a bitter smile.

'Let me tell you something nice. Just like that, pop', she said and she made a circle with her hands in the air, 'man invented soap. Yes, for someone like you.'

'Damn you', the woman spat the words through her teeth. 'You think you are smart, don't you? I'll...' She raised her hand to hit her, but Dana's cold look seemd to freeze her.

She left, clenching her fists, and slammed the door.

'I will surely not bring myself down to the level of this miserable woman, of this "nobody" ', she groaned.

A little later, Dana thought.

"Actually nobody is a "NOBODY". Any person means something. We are conceived by God. We have souls, and that's a big deal, even though not all of us are aware of that. Claudia and especially Vera may not know they have a soul. It's hard for me, really hard, to think what's in their minds. Hm, that's my positive side, but I'll hide it really well. She and I will be good friends. We'll talk a lot. It's strange that when it's just the two of us, when we actually talk, I feel good. My negative side doesn't offer me joy, but I still want her more. Maybe I'm crazy, I don't know.'

Dana finally fell asleep and didn't think of anything anymore.

In the night, the silence was so oppressive, as if it fell heavier than eternity on Dana's soul (whick had suddenly awakened). She was bathing in sweat, large beads were splashing her forehead and face.

'Where am I?' was her first thought and she touched the bed with crumpled sheets. Her hands were shaking a little.

She heard Vera's loud snoring and she suddenly seemed to wake up to reality.

Her lips crooked into a groan.

'Where could I be? How can I ask myself such questions? In Hell. I'll never leave it.' She looked towards the window behind her for a while, a minute or two, then she rushed to it, clinging firmly from the bars.

A bawl could be heard in the night.

'Aaah...' The girl's tears started flowing on her cheeks.

Vera woke up and narrowed her eyes, then she went back to sleep as if nothing had happened. She munched loudly. Dana didn't scream anymore, but her hands were stuck to the iron bars. She lowered her head, opened her lips, everything in her soul was falling down. Now, she was neither strong, nor bad. Now, she was Dana, with no feelings.

She turned her head when she heard the door open and saw the strip of weak light.

'What's the matter with you?', screamed the same fat nurse.

'Even in the night, my scream won't be heard', said Dana slowly, getting down from the windowsill.

'What?', said the woman amazed. 'Go to sleep immediately. I see that you've gone crazy.' She got out slamming the door.

Dana got under the thin blanket again. She cuddled and whispered, eyes closed.

"Even in the night, my scream won't be heard"

Ms. Ivan, the psychiatrist, sat comfortably on her chair, lined with vinyl. She was a beautiful blonde girl, with glowing blue eyes. She was older than 50, but she still seemed young.

Eric, the boy in the wheelchair, was looking at her smiling. He had always liked the doctress. She had listened to his opinions and helped him write a few pages. Eric read a lot and liked enumerating his own thoughts on white sheets of paper.

'Doctor, is it true that one person's suffering can't be compared to the suffering of others?'

The doctress smiled and crossed her legs.

'You're a clever boy, Eric. You want to know something, don't you?'

'It's my humble pleasure, but I can't boast about it too much. I am left-handed, at least I think so and I am not too educated.'

'Hey, think of Mark Twain. He only had 7 classes and tons of talent.'

'Mark Twain was Mark Twain.'

'And you are Eric', laughed the doctress. 'You can be better.'

'Ha, ha, ha', the boy laughed loudly, exposing his shiny white teeth.

'Good, you're laughing', said the woman, 'let's talk.'

She also liked talking to Eric. He was 24 years old, out of which 14 had been spent in orphanages, he had only 10 years of study, but he could be proud about that.

Eric always remembered that evening, like a well-known refrain, and just as ingrained in his mind. Snow had fallen abundantly, the mountain peaks were rising high, just like white statues, just like kings of the world. It was he and his parents. His dada was driving carefully (he had always been careful as much as he could not to hurt his family). He was driving slowly with his 4x4 Jeep, and was looking at the sign post from time to time. They were going up on a winding road, which was leading towards the chalet.

'Do bears live here?' The child's voice was thin and

nice. He had flattened his nose on the car window and was looking satisfied at the city which was lying down, lower and lower, like a fairytale view wrapped in multicoloured lights.

'Are there bears?', asked the child again.

His dad was too attentive to hear him, but his mom answered.

'Yes, baby, they can come down here as well, but they generally live in the heart of the mountains. But now they are hibernating. It's winter and it's cold.'

"They're hibernating", repeated the child, as if to himself and a smile appeared on his lips. Bears hibernate. Maybe he didn't understand, but he didn't really want to ask. Maybe he was, who knows? "Too clever." Hmm, a very clever 10-year-old boy.

Lots of cars drove past them, and the child was looking at the lights that were shining brightly, then slowly turning off in the darkness. It was wonderful. They would soon arrive at the chalet. There wouldn't be blinking lights there, but only the warm light in the fireplace. He didn't want to reach the destination. Eric, the child, wanted that the road trip would go on for ever, endlessly, and he would stay with his nose flattened on the window and count the lights. He suddenly turned, and with a slightly irritated voice, said:

'I want to go a long way.'

His mom and dad smiled.

'I don't want this journey to end. I want to see the lights.' He shut up for a moment. 'The lights that turn off in the darkness.'

A truck was coming from the opposite side. The man was laughing, the woman next to him was laughing, too.

Then everything got black. A thick and naughty

darkness. Eric woke up in the hospital with his hand and leg in plaster. A weak smile fluttered on his lips.

'Hello', the man said flatly.

The child'e eyes were blurry.

'Is the journey over?', he babbled.

The doctor nodded.

'Why?'

'Because...', the man looked up at the ceiling for a moment and tried to think about something.

'It's over because there was a lot of snow and the car got stuck.'

'And the lights?' The child's voice was strangled by tears. 'I didn't get to count all of them... Count them, count them, count them!!'

Doctress Ivan repeated.

'Let's talk. I see that your past is invading you again.'

Yes, the past was invading him, enveloping his mind, but strangely, he didn't feel pain anymore. He had felt it then, a long agony which traumatised his childhood for a long time. Suffering. Physical and soul pain. When he didn't feel his legs for the first time, there, in the hospital with shrivelled walls, he screamed, until he felt that his voice moved the clouds in the sky. And cried loudly, sighing deeply. 'I won't be able to play football' was his first thought. 'I won't enjoy it when the ball rolls in the air like a humming top'. He stared at the ceiling, and a strange, slightly excited smile appeared on his lips. The ball was up, rolling and entering the goal. Romania had given many footballers, and he would be one of them.

The woman was just looking at him, she didn't say

anything. Maybe she should take him out of metamorphosis, but she didn't. She waited for him to talk, but he didn't.

'Do you want to talk?', she finally asked.

His handsome face was immutable, like the face of a statue.

'Hm?' He shook his head as if thousands of water drops had drained from his hair.

She wrinkled her nose and narrowed her eyes. She was clever enough to realise that Eric had felt that "piece" of time again. Lia Ivan had been working for a long time at the hospital hospice, and was the first who saw the paralysed teenager, the glimpse of intelligence and kindness. But also suffering.

She had been talking a lot with him, for hours, and nights. She wasn't married, she didn't have any children, she lived alone with 6 cats. Eric appeared in her life and enlightened it. At first, it was a case study, then the patient-doctor relationship turned into a solid friendship. And Eric was happy. They were both dreamers, but also pretty rational. You can sometimes confuse reality with fantasy, but you must see reason. Wasn't it normal like that?

'Eric?' She looked at him frowning her eyebrows.

'Lia?', the boy laughed. It was a question.

Lia took a deep breath and smoothed the folds of the skirt. Outside, the day had become grey.

'I want to know something', she said, 'even if I seem ridiculous or absurd.'

He was looking at her and waiting.

'Are you happy?'

He closed his eyes, leaned back his head and seemed to immerse into a sweet dream. Then he said:

'Is it illogical to be happy in a prison?'

'I don't know... Forgive me, I am an idiot...'

He tried to make her believe that it wasn't like that.

'Certainly not, it's the right question, at the right place, don't blame yourself. I don't know, I just don't know. But a good feeling is invading me. And of tranquility', he added.

'Can you transmit this feeling?'

'I don't... I don't know what you want to tell me.'

'Eric, listen to me', said the doctress, 'I just want you to talk to someone.'

'And humanity will owe me', the boy laughed.

'I mean it, Eric. Do you know Dana?'

She had heard that a new girl would come. She wasn't like the others. What did it mean different than the rest? She wasn't crazy. But maybe the others weren't crazy either, maybe they lived in a world of their own. Just like autists. And some of them had no sphincter control. What nonsense she was thinking! Most of them were mentally retarded. Third, second and first degree oligophrenia. Should he understand that "the new one" wasn't mentally retarded? From what he had heard of, she wasn't.

'I didn't have the pleasure of meeting her. She doesn't eat when I do.'

'Yes, I know, but maybe...'

'No, I don't know her.'

'I want you to talk to her.'

He groaned.

'What am I, Lia? You are the psychiatrist.'

'I wanted you to talk to her before I do.'

The boy raised his eyebrows.

'You haven't talked to her yet!', he wondered.

'Yes, I have, but she didn't opened up to me and I have the strange feeling that she won't, either. She interiorises for a while, and then she explodes. You know, screams, nervousness, aggression. I know this from what the nurses have said. A brutal, unpolished aggression, Eric.'

Eric looked out of the transparent windows behind Lia. Who was he anyway? A poor disabled man, who had learned to sketch joy, quietness firstly, then really feel them. But he had cut his sheer aggression, leaving only the impulse to move forward. God empowered him by writing, his passion.

'Can I really help this girl? I haven't helped anyone in this orphanage, just myself. Maybe I am selfish. I want to feel peace, to be able to smile, look at others with mercy and try to snatch a tear. But I don't do anything to help them.'

'They won't open up their souls to me', he said coarsely, somehow upset with his own person because he had found out a dose of selfishness in himself and that right in the previous moment.

'Why do you think that?'

He looked intensely.

'I am selfish.'

She laughed slightly, took a Kent cigarette, lit it and smoked greedily.

'There is selfishness in each and everyone of us. I think this is how we are born. Haven't you noticed that even children are selfish? Would little Mickey give a toy to you or anyone else? You know very well that he wouldn't. He wants it for himself. And he is only four years old. What do you think?'

'Yes, you made me happy', said Eric ironically. 'I don't want to be selfish and yet I am. If my luck died, why should my neighbour's live? It's a strange feeling which I have never told you about. I am sometimes bad and I don't understand why. And I have also discovered that I am selfish as well.'

Lia exhaled the sour smoke towards the ceiling.

'Yes', she said. 'Let me tell you one thing. Each of us has got light and darkness, and if the lights are more and they shine, they almost blind you, then you can be happy. Light fades darkness away.'

Eric grabbed the wheelchair's wheels.

'I'm going into the ward.'

'All right', nodded Lia. 'It's your choice.'

A week had passed since Lia and Eric's conversation. The boy didn't know what to believe. On the one hand, he wanted to help the girl, on the other hand, he didn't know whether he were able to do that. 'I am not by far the peacemaker of the world.'

He saw Dana in the yard a couple of times, but he didn't dare talk to her. The girl was walking slowly in the paved yard, with her hands stuck in the pockets of her shorts, lost in thought. She would never smile, and if she did, she would do it sarcastically.

It started raining slowly. The sun had hidden behind a big grey cloud. She had laid the table, a pretty good potato dish, and a soup with lots of vegetables.

Dana was lying in bed, Claudia was sleeping, and Vera got up. She suddenly opened the door and got out into the hall. There the nurse was smoking.

'Go back to bed', she screamed.

Vera showed off a stupid smile, her saliva flowing

through her mouth as always, disgracefully. Being only in her underwear, her diaper had detached itself, and a part of it was hanging like a tail.

'Tete', said Vera and neared the nurse with her streched hand, with her crooked fingers.

She had pooped herself and she was stinking awfully.

Part of her excrements scattered on the stone floor. The woman writhed in horror. She was young and strong, and her eyes were gleaming with anger.

This damn work in this damn society which doesn't allow you to stick your head out. She had to wash these disabled women's excrements.

Vera neared her and touched her. Her fingers were wet with saliva. Then the woman saw red with anger. She smacked her strongly. She grabbed her by the sleeve of her cotton blouse, and with her other hand, pulled her hair.

'You damn disgusting woman', she gasped through her crooked teeth. She let her go for a moment, and Vera collapsed on the floor. Her lips curved and tears started flowing. Just about that, she didn't burst into tears. Vera would seldom cry and only when she got beaten really hard.

The nurse kicked her really hard and the girl lay on her back.

'Move!', screamed the nurse, as from the mouth of a snake. 'To the bathroom!'

Vera was looking at her through her canvas of tears.

'Move!' The woman's voice seemed hoarse with hatred. She hated the misery in which she was spinning. She hated disabled women.

'You're crazy', said a nurse from another ward, who had

come to drink a cup of coffee with her peer. 'If the manager sees you...'

'I know, I know', said the former woman.

Yes, she could be thrown out of the orphanage immediately, and her four children would be in distress. Her husband didn't earn much. She dragged Vera to the bathroom, she pushed her under the shower and had to wash her. Later on, she would bring her into the ward.

Dana was still lying in bed.

'Did you hit her again?', she said relentlessly.

'Shut up! This is none of your business.'

Dana got out of bed slowly. She neared the woman with an impenetrable face.

'Listen', she said, and the words seemed to roll out of her mouth, 'don't believe yourself the centre of the universe, 'cause you're not.'

The woman was sweating, putting some clean diapers on Vera. When she finished, she turned to Dana.

'Mind your own business!' Little beads of sweat covered her forehead. This girl is like a thorn in the butt.

Dana smiled ironically to her.

'Hm', she snorted, 'you'll see when the people from the department will kick you in the ass and you'll get out from the gate.'

The woman got up and held her loins. Her lips got thinner and turned into a grin.

'They'll believe you, won't they?'

Dana felt how the woman's voice was trembling a little and she aimed Achilles' heel.

'You bet on it.'

The woman thought for a few moments what explosion

it would be if they knew that these 'poor afflicted of fate' were being beaten by her. A wandering thought said: 'They'll believe the girl because she isn't crazy.' The latter said: 'But she is frustrated and restless and she can come up with anything'. 'Hm', said the former thought: 'It will be searched and Vera will have bruises all over her body. And the girl can try to prove it, she isn't stupid.'

There came the optimal solution – polish the girl. The woman suddenly turned more voluable, more conciliatory.

'You want to talk, don't you?'

Dana sat on the bed.

'Don't beat her anymore', she said, ignoring the woman's question.

'Let's be serious', whispered the woman, 'you also slap them once in a while.' The woman grinned as if she were an accomplice.

'I am crazy.'

The woman nodded and smiled foolishly.

'We are playing, aren't we?'

'I can do whatever I want. "They might take me straight to the grave from here, I don't think I'll be seeing my former orphanage", she thought.

'Why are you being so bad? Do you even care about Vera?'

The answer was 'no' or 'I don't know', but she said bluntly 'yes'. So, did she really care about Vera? She thought for a moment and remembered the lights and the dark parts in her inner self. There were moments when she couldn't care less about humanity, about her people, if she could, she would have thrown everybody in a cage, she would have locked the gate up and would have gladly taken the key away with her. Then she was proud of her fierce malice.

But there were moments, rare, to be honest, when she indulged in kindness and care towards the human being. Then she even liked skinny stray dogs and distempered cats. Then she cared about Vera. Had a glim just passed through her heart? Had she really cared for Vera or had she wanted to scare the woman? She didn't know it very well, but there would be nights when she was going to think about it.

The nurse sat on the bed next to Dana.

'You are a good girl, you know...'

'And you are so flattering. You are afraid, so afraid.'

Th woman was concise.

'Yes, I am. You don't have children to see how you feel when you have nothing to lay on the table.'

She shut up for a little while and then said.

'Stop playing with people's lives.'

Dana stood upright.

'You have no right to torture her like that. No right!', the young woman pointed at her in a threatening way. 'You have made her I don't know how many bumps on her head, bruises all over her body, of course not on her face, you have spilled enough blood on this dirty carpet.'

'Shut up!', the woman groaned, shaking.

Dana felt like she was supposed to be a little authoritative.

'Come on, get out. Call us for dinner.'

The woman snorted.

'You don't tell me what to do or else...', she then tempered her nervousness, thinking about consequences. "My little children". Am I crazy?" Maybe just as crazy as this poor sad woman who gives orders. Is it even normal to be given orders by her? She's blackmailing me with something. I am so stupid!"

She got out of the ward, leaving her pride aside.

'Am I really a happy man?', thought Eric, in his chamber as small as a box of matches. He had to live together with several colleagues (who were not sane at all, poor guys) in the ward, but Lia, the doctress, at Eric's request, got this chamber for him, because it had been a chamber before. It was cool both in the summer and in the winter, although the plumber had installed him a radiator. 'It's good',vthought Eric back then, 'I'll be able to relax here, meditate, reflect on the present, because the future can be very uncertain, I'll be able to write. It's wonderful! I'll be grateful to Lia for ever, although I sometimes blame myself for it. I have no right for this room, I am privileged. The others, poor guys, cannot be like me, and I, poor guy, cannot be like them.'

'Am I a happy man?', Eric asked himself again, lying in in bed, covered with a red blanket.

'Can I be happy in a prison?', he repeated an old thought. Happiness lies in each and everyone of us. We just have to find it, search deep inside our souls and take it out to light up our souls. Some people remain sad all their lives, because they didn't have the courage to search and find out. If everything shines around us, but there is rottenness inside, then depression erodes more than death. Strange, isn't it? "Strange are my thoughts, too", said Eric.

"I may be not happy, only a state of well being is surrounding my soul and this makes me the happiest. A divine drop has slipped into my being and has given me a lot hope." Eric thought about Dana. He saw her deep in thought, then, outside, in the yard, among the poor human beings. God can slip a divine drop in her soul, too. If only she wanted it! It would be wonderful!

The young man thought he had to talk to her, if only he could find the right moment for it!

Jimmy was no longer a boy. He was 20 years old, a wrinkled face, ruffled hair, and unusually blue eyes. He had mental retardation, not too severe, but he could sometimes do incredible things. One day, he put his hand in the cage where the teacher used to keep her parrot and then, grinning like a lunatic from the horror films, unveiling his vampire-like rugged teeth, stuffed it in his mouth. Incredible, but so true. Lucky that the teacher took it out by force from his mouth. The bird got its leg broken, some feathers were gone, and after a week, it died.

The woman scolded Jimmy, very upset.

'You're incredibly bad, Jimmy, you've practically killed the bird.'

As a reaction, Jimmy wanted to strangle her.

'You, stupid!', she groaned after she released herself from his squeeze. They were all the same. Between the dirty walls, worms were swarming.

The girls were masturbating each other so hard that no one was a virgin anymore. They stuck their fingers in their vaginas and grinned as if they were feeling a pathetic pleasure. In the hospital hospice, life seemed deformed, and reality couldn't be more striking.

Eric left his room and went up slowly on the hall paved

with cubic stone. It was raining heavily. Two 19 and 20-year-old boys were playing football with a smashed ball. Three girls were sitting against the wall and eating sunflower seeds, throwing the shells on the ground.

'Here comes Skinny Boy', said one of the girls. The other two were grinning.

'Stupid Skinny Boy. Ha, ha, ha.'

Eric ignored them and kept on spinning the wheels.

'My heart can never be weak', he thought. And these girls were as mad as a March hare. He smiled mildly thinking of it. Lia said it to him once when he entered her surgery upset.

'They all call me "Skinny Boy"', he said, with his eyes in tears. Lia laughed.

'All these "they" are as mad as a March hare. You have to sympathisise with them, not cry because of them. And if one of them called you so in front of the others, then the entire herd will. Just like sheep, do you understand?'

And he had understood. They were suffering, but weren't aware of it. When you are weaker, you unwillingly throw with dirt at the others so that you could feel strong. But the weakness remains and surrounds you like in a vise. All weak people (or almost all) are like this. All the more his so-called colleagues.

Eric kept on spinning the wheels of the wheelchair. He threw a fully compassionate look to the girls, who were still laughing and pointing at him.

'They're crazy and I must feel pity for them indeed.' Then he searched the doors of the wards and knocked at one door.

Dana was lying in bed, half asleep, and Vera and Claudia were sleeping.

'Hey, let me sleep', she screamed. 'Who is it?' "Some idiot, either a boy or a girl." She got out of bed.

'An idiot boy', she said opening the door. 'Disabled, disabled everywhere. I'll get intoxicated by disabled people.'

Eric smiled slightly.

'Are you Dana?'

Dana stared sarcastically at him.

'You can talk! Do you belong to the loose world?'

'Yes. And with bars.'

'Wow, but I haven't seen you around.'

'Well, I have. Can I come in?'

'Why?'

'I want to talk.'

Dana realised in amazement that the boy in front of her was sound-minded!

'Great, you're not insane!'

The boy's smile enlightened her face.

'Are you surprised?'

'Quite', she said quickly. The door was wide open. 'Come in and don't get embarrassed by these stinky girls.'

Eric spinned the wheels and entered looking around. How familiar was everything, shrivelled walls, stinky beds, the smell of stale air, the sour smell of disease.

Dana sat on the bed and, to her surprise, she realised she had been docile. Why? Because she had met the first normal person among afflicted people, hadn't she? Yes, that was it. She would usually speak to no one, and if she did, she had to be sarcastic or aggressive. And she was sometimes right.

Just like when the nurse had beaten Vera soundly. Ironic and devastating.

'Listen', she said pouting. ' I don't know what made me have you in my castle. I think you are sound-minded.' Eric laughed.

'Haven't you seen sound-minded people before?'

'Oh, yes, I have', said Dana, 'but not from our "group". And now, come on, what do you want from me?'

Eric thought for a moment, calmly.

'Come on, you don't say.' She bent towards him. 'Could it be love at first sight?'

Eric became sad all of a sudden.

'I am not allowed to fall in love,' he whispered, as if to himself. 'I am not allowed to.'

Dana closed her eyes and nodded.

'I want to sleep', she said all of a sudden, 'and you are taking away my precious time.'

Eric thought of pushing it a little, gently, but firmly.

'Don't you want to talk to me?'

'Who are you so that I would talk to you?'

'Maybe a future friend, even though a "skinny" one'. He called himself 'skinny' unwillingly, just like the others were calling him. The didn't like the word at all, but he was just a paralysed boy. Damn it, he considered himself a victim, and that was not good at all.

He coughed and remembered why he was there.

'Let's sum up', he said displaying a sincere sympathy for the girl in front of him, 'I want to talk.'

Dana snorted, avoiding his words.

'I am disgusted by everything that's here, look at them', she said, opening her arms and pointing at Claudia and

Vera, 'they sleep, poop, eat or vice versa. We live a poor life. When I say "we", I mean you and I.'

She smiled bitterly and then went on.

'I don't know whether I am too healthy or not, but anyway I am aware of where I am. I am aware of pain. This is not good. They,' and she pointed again at the girls who were sleeping, 'live in a world where everything is pink. We don't.'

She seemed to be talking alone, her thoughts were miles away.

'I know I am a wreck and I will be for the rest of my life.'

Eric moistened his lips and nodded that he had understood her. And he believed that once. The ground was opening and closing on him, and he hardly had an ounce of strength to scream or struggle.

His luck was Lia. And he... he will be Dana's luck. 'So help me God', he said in silence.

'It will be all right', he said just as calmly. And he really believed that at the present moment.

Dana suddenly got up.

'I want you to leave', she said, hiding her irritation. 'You're a stupid boy, come on, get out. I can still keep my nerves under control. You are also a silly boy.'

Eric grabbed the wheels and slowly opened the door, then left. He didn't actually expect to win from the first. The pain in the soul is the most unbearable, and people abandon themselves in it, because they are afraid to fight. And Dana was afraid to fight. Sometimes, in those states of deep depression and restlessness, he felt like doing something bad, really bad. He allied himself with those instincts and wished that the entire planet Earth would disappear. When his mind and soul were clear, he would hug everybody, smiling brightly.

He had to work on it, so that he could melt the darkness in it. And he thought how hard it had been to do it. He couldn't ask anything from Dana now, not even a few words said at the right time. No, not even that.

Nina woke up crying. She had dreamt about Dana, she was next to her, to her bed and was singing something nice to her. Then she disappeared, fading slowly, leaving in a place known only by her.

'Mommy', screamed the girl through heartbreaking tears. 'My good mommy! I miss her so much!'

She got out of bed and looked through the window. The sky was covered by clouds, without stars. She whispered slowly: 'Mommy'. Her cheeks were wet with tears.

She opened the door and closed it back so that she would not wake the girls up (Stella slept in the same room with her), and with bare feet, got out in the hallway. Two nurses were standing at the window, talking, smoking and drinking coffee.

'What's the matter with you, honey? The sun isn't up yet.'

Nina passed by them, practically not hearing them. 'God, help me, I want to see her. I will lose my tranquility if my mommy doesn't caress my forehead for a long time.'

She entered Bianca's room. The door was open. Ms. Boobs was snoring, lost in who knows what dreams.

'Bibi, Bibi', said Nina, shaking the young woman. She knew very well that Ms. Boobs couldn't stand her, but she had no choice. Maybe she had to ally herself with the enemy until she found peace.

Ms. Boobs munched, rubbed her armpit and mumbled something.

'Bibi', insisted the girl, and went on. 'Bibi, wake up.'

Bibi startled and opened her eyes half asleep.

'Hey', she said. 'What the hell are you doing here, you freak?'

'You can call me anything, just help me.' Nina's eyes filled with tears again. 'I want to see her', she sighed, pulling Bianca.

'Go away. Come on, go away', groaned Ms. Boobs and pushed her. 'I want to sleep. Who do you think you are to wake me up in the middle of the night?'

'I am nobody, but listen to me.'

Ms. Boobs sighed.

'What?'

'I want to see her.'

'Your grandmother?'

'No, Dana.'

Bibi grinded her teeth, then hesitated. Even though she she had been bad, Dana had meant something for her. She had helped her get rid of Joe, had given her pizza (to be honest, with the money begged by her) and... had ... sometimes... been ... good.

'Do you know how to get there?', said Nina slightly excited, seeing Bianca's silly face. If she had screamed like crazy, then her desire would have been in smoke, but Bianca's face showed some emotion.

'Yes, I think so', nodded Bibi.

Nina smiled gladly.

'Shall we go tomorrow?'

'Yes, I think so.'

Nina did something she had never done before. She kissed Ms. Boobs noisily on her cheek. She was so excited. She will finally see Dana. She left, already feeling the tranquility flowing like a lava in her body. And it was so good! She went to sleep thinking about daylight.

And Bibi? Bibi was deep in thought. The little girl could also be nice. That's why Dana loved her. And nobody had ever kissed her before (not even the Italians who were supposed to come and soothe their pain).

She'll see Dana and she won't know what to tell her. Had she been glad that she had left? Had she been bad, had she had outbursts of frail joy? Bibi somehow felt guilty. She rarely had feelings of guilt and when she had, it wasn't comfortable at all. Did she feel good when she was bad? She thought a little, then she decided. Sometimes she did, other times she didn't. She was a bad girl and a good girl as well. Two people in one.

Loudly, imperatively, Dana's words suddenly seemed to resound in her ears: 'Save me!'

But what could such an insignificant person like her do? Nothing, absolutely nothing. She put her head on the pillow and couldn't notice the fact it felt good to be good.

Mid-September was clear and mild. A warm sun was shining during the day and rusty leaves were swept away by a quiet wind.

To Dana, the day started to look dull, bleak, just like the others. She was sitting outside, on the gnawed stone bench, when, among the greasy young people who were walking in the yard, there she was. How foolish, of course, what was her little girl doing in this fortress? She was afraid not to go insane. Could she go insane, just like that, all of a sudden? Of course she could. Frustrations gathered and the outbursts were too few.

'Mother!'

The girl's scream, who was nearing quickly, made Dana's heart beat fast and somehow see that is was real. When she turned, Nina was in front of her, and next, they hugging tightly and crying.

'You shouldn't have come here. Here everything is black.'

'I don't want you to see me die', screamed Dana's inner voice. But she was very glad to see her. She had been dreaming about her so many times and just as many times she had been crying. She sometimes felt guilty towards "her girl" because she behaved abnormally once. Those weren't her true feelings, but she gave vent to her instinct and was wrong. But she didn't have to think about that anymore. Her filthy past won't invade her mind anymore.

She was still holding Nina tightly in her arms and kissing her cheeks, when she saw Bianca.

Strange feelings were invading her, she had suddenly shaken off the whole darkness that had been invading her soul, the wickedness that she had been displaying for just a few times. A state of pity, of love was crossing her heart, making her feel a "good" person.

'Bibi', she whispered, as if more to herself, with tears on her cheeks.

Ms. Boobs was staring at her as if to a wonder. Never

ever had Dana cried. She was bad and strong. She was bossy. Dana stretched out her hand, but Bibi stood still as if hypnotised.

As if she had read her mind, Dana said:

'You know another side of my soul, Bibi. Is it hard to accept this?'

'Well, well, ...yes', said Bibi flat.

Dana laughed.

'Hey, come on.'

Bibi came closer, and Dana also hugged her tightly. She had also been missing Ms. Boobs with her foolishness and all, she had been missing all that universe where she had become "the boss". She didn't know that the manager, that grey-haired old lady would take such a restrictive measure. Living in the hospital hospice is like living in hell.

The girls stayed for more than an hour, told Dana what was going on at the centre, how were things at the Child Protection (not to good, as they didn't have enough clothes) and waited for her to tell them as well.

'Here, everything is "nothing", even life itself', said Dana. It was all she said about the hospice hospital and was sure that the girls understood.

She couldn't say more, without feeling like she was going to throw up. Bibi and Nina left, and Dana didn't feel sad anymore, she felt glad. The day seemed to have become brighter, the sky didn't seem to be covered with clouds anymore. There will come a day when she will shine brightly with happiness. She will leave hell, somewhere far away, maybe, who knows, with Mario and Nina (she will definitely take her as well).

It was lunchtime, a lot of bread and a lot soup. Dana

would have felt like spitting just like old times if her stomach hadn't rebelled from hunger. She broke some bread, softened it in the soup and that was how she ate three slices. She got up and got out in the hall. She didn't throw away any chair, because she was in a good mood. She had just seen Nina and nothing would have ruined her day. She went into her room, lay in bed, and with her eyes on the ceiling she smiled brightly, a true serene smile without any trace whatsoever of skepticism. She was happy. Simple, yet at the same time, complex. Can you be happy here, between these cold and tough walls? Never, she had once answered her own question. Since she came to the hospital hospice, she had only seen the grey of life, the dirty transitory world, the restlessness in which some people struggle. And not just some people, the whole world, in fact. Even if they don't admit it, people live their lives in stages. Joy, sadness, well being, sickness, happiness (who knows if there really is happiness?) That was what Dana was thinking about now, she could synthesize things (or so she said) and she could also see life much better. She felt really good and if this state of wellness was called happiness, then she was happy, as she thought. What else mattered? Everything was fine.

She finally fell asleep, really quietly and calmly. When she woke up, after two hours, she was still in a good mood and started laughing really noisily, seeing Vera in the middle of the room, chewing diligently a green linen slipper. Vera stopped for a moment and grinned.

'You're so pretty. And you've also peed on you', noticed Dana.

'Pee...pee', spelt Vera.

'Sure, yours. But you know, I am not going to bother

the nurse, who's drinking coffee. Come on, sit down there and eat your slipper slowly.'

Dana jumped out of bed, took out of the wardrobe a white cotton blouse, a towel, a pair of lace underwear and left, slamming the door.

'Keep calm, don't bother', she said ironically to the nurse who was drinking coffee and smoking near the window.

Dana had a hot bath, rubbing herself until her skin turned red. She was amazed that the water was actually boiling.

She entered her room again, meanwhile the nurse had changed Vera and she smelled horribly of urine.

'Wonderful!', said Dana.' But of course I can't be upset, but I can't stay either.' She looked the nurse straight in the eye.

'Where shall I go? I haven't got any friends here.'

Then she thought, closing her eyes halfway.

'I think I ... actually have someone, but I am not too sure. Where does the boy in the wheelchair stay?'

The nurse snorted.

'Honey, all of them are in a wheelchair here.'

'The sound-minded one.'

'There aren't any sound-minded people here.'

Dana left babbling.

'All right, and you are stupid.'

She was looking out of the open window, with bars. It was getting dark, the daylight was losing ground. The sun was setting quietly.

Two weeks had passed since Nina and Bianca came, but

she called the centre. She asked the kind doctress nicely, and she helped her. She wasn't upset. Nina promised she would come again. Her visits will drown her pain and she will go on, even though she didn't know where she was headed.

She felt a hand on her shoulder and turned, but not suddenly. She was glad to see him.

'Are you just passing by?', she smiled.

'No', said Eric. 'I've come to you.'

She pointed at him, scolding him and smiling.

'I'll be mad at you, bad boy. You didn't want to hear anything about me. How come?'

He noticed in amazement.

'You're changed!' But he couldn't possibly know that she was so moody. Agony, next enthusiasm, and then vice versa.

'In what way? I seem more lively, don't I?'

'I've never pretended that you've died'. She smiled gently once again.

'Why are we here anyway?'

'Have you ever thought that this is the very place where we can find each other?'

'No, not this, it's nonsense! Everything around is rotten, and you want me to daydream about you, thinking about you.'

She stood for a moment, thinking.

'I actually think about you, you know.'

'See? So, not everything is lost. Come on', he said, stretching his hand out, 'we'll be all right in my chamber.'

"The ice is melting. That's great! And I wouldn't have imagined it so soon... It took me even longer", thought Eric. It means that he's been persuasive, and her life couldn't be simply imputed.

In a few minutes, they were in Eric's chamber or little room.

'Sit on the bed, the chair is shaky. They brought it so that I could just lean on it when I lie in bed.'

Dana measured the entire room with her eyes. It was narrow and cool, but he was probably feeling good, because he was sharing it with anyone.

'It smells like mould', she said, finally sitting on the bed.

He laughed gently.

'Tell me something that doesn't smell of anything in this place? Even people have their own particular smell.'

'Well, yes', concluded Dana.

'Come on, tell me, what's with this joy that I can feel in your body and soul?'

'It's no big deal. I am warning you, I am a bad person, but I love somebody very much. This person visited me some time ago and I realised one very important thing. I am loved. My story is simple. I don't belong to anybody, so I didn't expect anybody to love me. However, I don't know how much it will last. The dual tension within me will know how to impose itself. I will become bad again, when I least expect it.'

'And what does malice mean?'

'Pain, a lot of pain.'

'You want to suffer.'

'Don't be naughty!', she shouted. 'I don't want to suffer, I don't want to be bad.'

'You're lying, malice sometimes keeps you in a good shape. Are you denying that it gives you pleasure?'

She thought about Bianca. She had made her suffer a lot, she had ordered her bluntly to do things which were not too desirable, she had adventured to be "the boss". She laughed like crazy, she was bad, but paradoxically, she didn't like it.

'Yes, I deny it', she groaned.

'All right, come on, calm down. I want to help you, nothing more. You have a beautiful face and you could earn a lot.' She seemed to be thinking about it, then she said.

'Do you want me to thank you?'

'For what?'

'Maybe because you appreciate me. Oh, I don't know what to think about you. I don't know you and yet it seems like I have known you forever.'

'Is it possible that our souls attract each other, feel attracted to one another? I repeat, only our souls.'

She laughed out loud for a few moments.

'Maybe, maybe. I am in a good mood and I wouldn't like to contradict you. You do know. Are you afraid of an indecent assault?'

'No, I'm afraid that you'd think I'd want that.'

'OK, OK', she said, 'are you afraid that I'm going to consider you a man? Well, you don't know much about me. Maybe, who knows, there'll come a time when I might tell you more. Then you'll be totally amazed.'

Nina paid Dana a visit again. She had learnt the way. But this time, her protectress was sad.

'Has something happened? Aren't you happy to see me?', asked Nina worried.

Dana caressed her gently on her head.

'I think you shouldn't worry. You are everything to me. Just that I am worried about the prison.'

'Prison?'

'Yes, where I live. The days drag one after the other, and I am only waiting for the end.'

Nina was looking at her with a devouring look, a frightening curiosity.

'I know, I know, I don't understand anything. I'm going to die here, Nina. I just want you to cry on my deathbed, and right now I would really like to touch your angel face.' The girl rushed to Dana's chest and cried out loud for a few minutes.

Dana looked far away in the distance. They were outside, on the concrete bench.

'Cry, let it all out, my little girl.' She felt like an woman who was making a tragedy out of her life, as if begging for affection. Why was she doing that? She really had Nina's entire affection just for her. The girl was all hers. Heart and soul. Dana knew that she was being selfish, and she hated herself for that, but she felt that instinctively. She shouldn't torment Nina.

She finally said:

'Come on, go, the teacher will be looking for you.'

'You won't die, will you?'

'I will live forever.'

'You won't die, will you?', Nina repeated the question, not understanding anything from what Dana was saying.

'Come on, go, honey.'

Nina left, turning her head from time to time. 'She won't die', shouted her thoughts. 'No!'

The following night, Dana fell in a deep and exhausting sleep, just like that of the hepatic patients. No trace of dreams, to destroy her subconscious and her night peace.

She woke up in the morning and went to the bathroom. She looked in the mirror and saw a face subjugated by evil pain.

"I can't live in prison. Everything in me has broken into pieces. The state of mind of being "a boss", the malice infiltrated in my entire being, the indignation, which seemed to give me an impulse towards life. I am not bad anymore, but not good either. I am a void, crossing the planet for a while. I don't want this anymore. I don't want to be a void anymore, I don't want to live in "between". I am not crazy, but I can't call myself sound-minded either. But still, it's a tragedy to live among insane people. I want to die."

She headed towards the kitchen.

'Could you give me some bread?'

'It's not meal time yet', said the skinny cook.

'Well, yes, but I'm hungry.'

'Just wait a little.'

'Sure, how can I not?'

She seemed like she was tripping. She was touching the air with her bare feet.

'I can't live anymore.'

She ran into him on the hallway.

'Good morning', said Eric smiling. She saw his face and her soul trembled.

'Do you really think it's good?'

'Yes, all of them are good. You just have to repeat it to yourself every day.'

'I'm hungry.'

'Let'go eat.' He stretched out his hand. 'Come on, I've got a sponge cake in the drawer.'

She smiled sadly and followed him.

'Take a seat.'

Dana sat on the bed as if she was sleepwalking. He grabbled and took out a piece of fresh sponge cake, in cellophane. He handed it to her.

'Lia gave it to me. When her mother cooks something good, she brings a little to me, too.'

Dana weighed it in her hands. Her eyes suddenly filled with tears.

'I feel terrible. Here you are, I don't want anything anymore. I was wrong. I am not hungry, I don't know how to handle my senses. I am useless and bitter. My soul is bitter, my peace is torn apart.'

'I know', he said simply.

"But the world doesn't end here. And don't wait for the impossible without moving a finger."

It was late autumn, a huge warm sun in the sky.

'Get up. We're leaving.'

Her smile was bitter just as it was sad.

'You're crazy. The fortress will never open its gates. And the walls are damn thick. And maybe ...', he suddenly said, maybe I am tired of dreaming anymore. Me, far away from the unleashed world.' Dana thought for a moment.

"I've changed, I can feel it, I don't like changes, though it weren't me anymore. I change myself and I think that my safety (my frail safety) disappears. My mind's paths are really winding. Where are my ironic smile and my authoritative attitude? My depression is the only one left, like a rigid rock, which will remain forever."

'Get up!'

'What else is left for me to do?', she said, going on aloud with her string of thought.

"SUICIDE. That's it. The road to nowhere sealed with precious stones. Eric leaned towards the young woman.

'What else is left for you to do? Is this what you're asking? Well, a short walk. I'll be back quickly. Do you promise me that you'll wait for me here?'

'I never promise anything to anybody.'

'When you want, you know how to be nasty. Promise me!', he shouted.

She opened her mouth to say something, but closed it back.

'Promise me!'

She nodded automically.

Eric came back with a leave of absence from Lia. This woman was wonderful. He would have done anything for her.

'I want to do something for Dana', he said, 'and you must help me.' He told her brierfly about the girl's condition, and Lia smiled.

'Never forget to be kind.' She was happy.

Dana hadn't left the hospital hospice since she came. She was punished. The other youngsters got out from time to time accompanied by the teacher. Eric also got out with Lia, the doctress always looking out for him like a guardian angel. They went to symposiums, to the theatre and to the park. They sometimes just stayed outside and admired how the snowflakes fell from the sky.

Now, Eric waved the leave of absence in front of Dana.

'Come on, we're going for a walk.'

She smiled nervously.

'I am punished', she said flatly.

'Now you're not.'

A warm wind was blowing. The sun was shining brightly on them.

She was contemplating, stunned.

'What are you doing?', said Eric.

'I am looking at the world. This is the huge privilege I am happy about at the moment.'

Her face changed. A slight redness was colouring her cheeks. Eric didn't know whether the girl was happy or not, whether the sadness had vanished even a little bit or not.

'How long do you think I'll be punished? Forever?'

Eric laughed hearing her.

'I'm glad to hear you talk like that.'

'You're crazy.'

'Don't repeat yourself. You've already said that.'

'Why are you happy?'

'I am happy for you, for your heart and soul.'

'You know, you're such an idiot.'

'OK. Do you know that you have never ceased to hope? Do you know that you want to fight, but you are repressing this right? Seeing the sky, you want to be free. Now you feel how life is pulsating and you don't want to die.'

She looked at him indignantly.

'How do you know how I feel?'

"The alliance of the mentally suffering people. Death, life, a more or less distance!"

'I guess.'

'I don't want you to guess anything anymore.'

He was looking at the children who were playing in the sand, in front of him, then he said:

'Tell me that at least now you like the sky.'

'I can see the sky every day when I get out in the yard.'

'Look', he said and raised his arm, with his index finger up, 'it is clear now. Not one cloud, nothing, just cloudlessness.'

Dana also looked up.

'That's right, the sky is clear.' A mild smile brightened her face. 'I want you to know that ... it's OK.'

The wrinkle between Eric's eyebrows betrayed his distrust.

'Stop looking at me like this. It's true.'

'Like this, just a little, isn't it?'

'Yes, don't expect a miracle.'

'It's a miracle what you're feeling right now.'

'A little freedom can move mountains.'

"I know that I have my limits, that I can't ask from myself for something I don't have. Maybe the will to pull out from my chest this conglomerate of images and negative states. I have a fickle, a controversial way of thinking, as if sometimes ferocious with me as well. I don't know what I want, I am not even sure if I want to be happy. Maybe happiness scares me, I don't know."

They stayed for a while, frozen in time. They talked about their lives, about the light and darkness within themselves. They talked about themselves. There followed several days in a row, staying together in his chamber and listening to the poignant sound of winter.

It was snowing now and then and Dana was feeling good. She felt good with Eric.

Nina came one day, also accompanied by Bianca and brought a letter from Mario.

'You are happy, aren't you?', said Nina enthusiastically.

Dana smiled. Mario remembered her once in a while. She would have been happy some other time, but now it was just the smell of a bygone joy. She didn't understand why and she didn't want to know too much. That was what she was feeling then and that was it.

The daily routine was unaltered. The meals, the morning, the noon, the evening, the staff in a continuous back and forth, quietness, unquietness, aggression, non-aggression.

Dana still lived with Vera and Claudia, who didn't progress at all.

During the day, she stayed with Eric. The young man had given her some books to read, which the girl finally accepted. She was nervous one day, it was snowing heavily, which made her sad.

'I'm not feeling well', she told Eric, as if wanting to find some kind of diagnosis to her symptom.

He was also depressed. He blamed it on the weather.

'Yes, and what do you want from me?'

She took a book from the table and threw it at him.

'You, bastard! I don't need your miserable books. I thought that...', Dana bit her lips because of her anger.

He sat upright nervously (he had been lying in bed) and screamed for the very first time.

'Stop victimizing yourself, you are brave enough. Do you hear me?'

She stared at him hypnotized.

'Yes, I do', she said flatly and left.

He broke the glass of water and dozens of pieces of glass scattered on the floor. He then sighed deeply, not censoring his sigh.

'You're a jerk', said the young man aloud. 'A stinking shit.'

"Come on, don't try walking on the steep slope again", screamed one of his thoughts. "You know how hard it is to climb it."

"I know, I know, but I want to save her, and what am I doing?"

"You're just being you, you have the right to make mistakes, because that's human nature."

'I have the right to make mistakes, but what I want most is to have the right to herself.'

There was a hard frost at night. The wind was blowing heavily, as if wanting to send a message to the average mortals. "I am stronger than you, my own voice sometimes horrifies you. It sounds macabre."

Vera and Claudia were sleeping. It was warm in the room. The room was being extremely heated like never before. It was Dana's first winter at the hospital hospice.

She couldn't sleep and started thinking. She had read a book for the first time, 'The Two Dianas', by Dumas, and she also heard for the first time about Nostradamus, the famous predictor. She felt superior to many and she felt that she had finally been reformed. She had never thought that she could be reformed, she wasn't ready for that. Eric had done a miracle. She smiled sweetly. It meant a lot to her.

She got up all of a sudden, put on her training suit, and wearing a pair of fluffy slippers, without any socks, she then got out slowly.

Two nurses were smoking in the hallway, as usual.

'Where are you going?', asked one of them, sounding completely uninterested though.

'To pee, then I want to breathe some fresh air in the yard.'

'Some frozen air, honey.'

The women went on gossiping, smoking and drinking black coffee.

Dana slowly climbed down the stairs and headed towards Eric's chamber. She knocked twice slowly.

'Are you sleeping?', she whispered. "No, he was playing poker by himself at three o'clock in the morning."

'Eric?'

The boy was sound asleep, covered with a thin blanket. He didn't feel her. She sat on the bed. Just like he was sleeping, Eric seemed a child who was waiting for his mother's mild touch.

And she... she will be his mother now.

She put her hand on his warm forehead, caressed his hair, and a few seconds later, he opened his eyes slowly. The light outside flashed through the room wrapped in the darkness of the night.

'What are you doing here?', he said hoarsely.

'Sssh. I've come to see you.'

He closed his eyes, took her hand and touched his hot lips with it.

'Forgive me!'

'Oh, stop blaiming yourself. I am the jerk here. But let's not talk about all these anymore, they do much harm.'

She got under the blanket next to him.

Eric sighed.

'Why are you doing this to me?', he said, sparing himself of any effort at all of pushing her away from him.

In response, she licked his lips, tarrying her tongue on them. He moaned.

'No, it's unfair.'

'Is it unfair that I touch you?'

Dana raised her arms and took off her training jacket and her T-shirt. Her breasts were nice and firm, and he felt like his eyes were being cobwebbed. He wanted to resist her, but he wasn't able to. He was way too fascinated.

'Look at me', said Dana.

He quickly moistened his lips. His heart was beating fast, as if it were coming out of his chest.

The girl came nearer and took off his T-shirt. Her eyes widened in astonishment. Eric was really well-built. Muscular, even though he hadn't done any sports.

'You're gorgeous.' She started kissing his nipples, her tongue then exploring his chest.

He closed his eyes again voluptuously. Never had he had such sensations, which were distorting his entire being. He touched her breasts with shaky lips, feeling as if he were choking with pleasure. So much pleasure, so much joy and restlessness at the same time. Will he be able to handle what's next? He was trying not to think about it, anyway he didn't have an ounce of strength to step away. A little later, they made love, Dana on top of him, touching his intimate parts with so much love. In the end, both of them shook with pleasure.

Dana collapsed on his chest, then a little later, their eyes met. His eyes were full of tears. He was crying.

'Oh, I wish I hadn't made you suffer. No, not this.'

Eric was breathing intermittently. He was caressing her face with his sweaty hand.

'Why did you do this?'

She threw back her head and smiled, fully satisfied.

'A small part of what you have given me.'

'A small part of my life, maybe even more, much more.'

'Do you want to talk about this? I think it's pointless.'

Dana lay in bed next to him. They were both naked.

'I am happy. I am happy now. How about that?'

'I am stunned, astonished. I can't describe anything, I just can't. I want to know, for you, did it mean ... joy?' His voice was trembling with fear.

If so, then I will breathe a sigh of relief for the rest of my life. And that's because I want you to be happy. Nothing compares with happiness, not even the humble, but so much more wished for joy.'

She took his hand and put it where the heart beats fast.

'It has never been like this, like crazy. I was steadfast and I knew how to take life's blows. Not always, to be honest, but... Believe me, I don't know what to say. I am ... euphoric.'

'The thought itself is dazzling.'

'You knew how to sneak in me, and this means a lot. You haven't done this before, have you?'

He was staring at the ceiling, dazzled.

'I am sorry, I am such a fool.'

'No, don't say this. Who would have even looked at a disabled man? I want you to know something. I didn't start talking with you for an infamous purpose, I just wanted to...'

Before he went on, she put her finger on his lips. She was so confident now, like never before.

'What we are doing now, what we have felt is not by far infamous. Do you really believe this?'

'I just think... "I LOVE YOU" ', screamed a thought, as if at the top of his lungs.

"She'll leave and you'll stay here, missing her like crazy and heartbroken. The demons of the past will come up again, they'll enfetter you like huge snakes. You won't be able to chase them away."

Dana kissed him again. Then she caressed his cheek tenderly.

'Nobody can ever know when pain turns up. I just know that I want to live my life, every minute of it, every second of it. Joy, sadness, agony, then ecstasy. I don't want to die.'

'I don't want to die either', he said, amorously. In such notice, you have become the axle (metaphorically speaking) I propped my life on.

Had her irrational attitudine disappeared or had it just hidden in a corner, where it could come out bluntly?'

'My world had been unhealthy until you came up. "What's the matter with me? I am talking as if he were the centre of the universe, my whole world, my system of values, my own genitor. All of a sudden, true values have come out from my mind. This change scares me, it creates a strange feeling, but joy surrounds me at the same time, making me taste life."

Eric looked at her with a radiant amazement.

'I want to believe what you're saying, I really want it.'

She weighed her thoughts in an imaginary balance.

"Is it true what I am saying or is it just the illusion of the moment? Am I really happy? Have I changed?"

"You have to find your own answers."

'Let's not think about all these. True feelings will come to light, but they need time.'

'That's true, time will solve everything. I want you to know something. I will never forget this night, but I won't ask you for anything. The only thing that interests me is that you're happy. Be happy, even in prison. Nobody can impede you.'

She nodded.

'That's true.'

She got up slowly, she cast one look toward the boy and left.

Christmas came. The youngsters from the hospital hospice, the nurses and the teachers decorated the fir trees with colourful lights. Eric and Dana met daily and behaved like old friends. Dana felt like shaking off the memories and the ghosts of the past. They didn't make love anymore. It seemed like in those moments of ecstasy something had broken apart, but it had also bonded between them.

It was evening, and the little bulbs lit for the first time. Lia came to Eric's room, where Dana was, too.

'Come and see the lights', she said enthusiastically. 'The whole world is smiling at us.'

A little later, Lia, Eric and Dana were looking at the little lights which where shining in the masked darkness. They were looking at the LIGHT.

'Let's go back in', said Dana. 'I'm cold. We can look at the lights in the fir trees from the hallway.'

Lia climbed up the stairs, towards the surgery, and the

two young people remained near the Christmas tree. Dana sat on the sofa, and Eric in the wheelchair, next to her.

'I am Dana', said the young woman, filled with effusion. 'I am Dana. It's a miracle. I just want to be Dana. My free and intimate voice says this.'

He looked at her startled as if he wanted to say "Are you crazy?"

'No', laughed Dana, 'I'm talking nonsense, forgive me.'

'Please, tell me', he said.

'Do you think there's something to tell?'

'Of couse there is.'

Dana got up from the sofa and came closer to the window. It started snowing and she smiled. Then she turned towards him and sat back on the sofa. A little farther, down the hallway, a few troubled youngsters were smoking greedily and laughing. Jimmy was also among them. Jimmy, the lunatic.

'You think I'm crazy, don't you?'

'I don't know', he said frankly.

She looked at the snow, at the big snowflakes, and said:

'I was also an actress, you know? I have also played some parts. Characters that have marked my life and have made others believe that I am completely out of my mind.

Eric was listening to her, without asking any questions. She just had to go on. And she did.

'I was Cristina, Elena, Denisa, Dorothy. Just like in "The Wizard of Oz". You know what's surprising? These names belong to four pretty girls. They lived a normal life, they had a house of their own or lived with their parents, had boyfriends whom they made love with, met different people. I endeared them. Who are they? They were my teachers throughout time. I wanted to be like them from the bottom of my heart. I loved their identity. So I stole it from them. In my intimacy, I lived through them. It sometimes filled me with joy, other times, it just pushed me towards suicide. Why? Because I was so fake and I was asking for too much. Thoughts were interweaving in my mind and I was falling into a bad depression. I had a fate worse than death. Do you believe me?'

Eric took her hand.

'Yes, I do.'

'And there's something else. Death. When I am afraid of it, I deplore that of others, when I am strong and I ignore it, then I also ignore the death of the entire humanity.

'You're a complex person.'

'So complex that I can't understand myself either.'

Eric laughed.

'To your surprise, I think I understand you.'

She rushed to him and hugged him.

'You're wonderful, wonderful, wonderful.'

It was New Year's Eve. The hospice's staff offered the festivity hall to the youngsters. They decorated it with a lot of tinsel, a Christmas tree with artificial snow was throning in one corner and lots of food. Sweets, steaks and alcoholic drinks.

Dana was wearing (as ever) a long black dress, and Eric some grey suiting trousers and a blue shirt just like his eyes.

The music started playing very loudly and the youngsters were trying a sort of dance of theirs, a little crazy, like some jitter of afflicted people. Nevertheless, they were happy, just like that, in their own world, where the conscience that you're different than the others disappears. But which human being totally resembles another one? There are both great distances and approaches between people.

Jimmy was sitting on the chair and munching an apple. He had refused to get dressed festively and was wearing a greasy training suit. He was tall, very tall and very ill. Two teachers and a nurse were chatting and looking after the youngsters from time to time.

'I'd like to dance', said Dana to Eric.

The young man took her hand to his lips.

'I'd like to watch you', he said, smiling faintly.

Dana bent over and looked him in the eye, as if he wanted to send him a message.

'With you', she said flatly.

He lowered his head and closed his eyes. Humility disarmed him.

'Hey?', said Dana, lifting his chin with her finger.

'I don't like this joke', he said, as if looking beyond her.

'On such a wonderful night, when the sun is shining within us, do you think I am joking on account of your infirmity? Plus, I think you're happy. I believe this is what you've said, isn't it? "You can be happy in a prison." Come on, give me your hand. You have given me a lot, I also want to make up for all that. And I am doing it with all my heart, you know.'

He believed her now. He saw it in her eyes and felt it in her voice that she was telling the truth. God, was it possible that... he left the thought pending somewhere in his mind. He was free to think, to dream, to hope.

He stretched out his hand and she took in his hand, smiling.

The music was festive, more rhythmical, so that the youngsters could frolic at will.

Eric started moving the wheels of the wheelchair and spinning around, Dana was taking a bow once in a while, touching his face. She was spinning around, raising her hands just like a ballerina. It was only their dance, no one else's, even though the music was quite agitating, they were dancing slowly, dreaming.

Dana was laughing, and Eric's eyes were full of tears. He had never danced since the accident, and he wouldn't have ever thought about ever being able to do that again. It was a miracle that he had done it. They danced all night, just like that, in that atypical rhythm, with an almost stubborn will. But they felt good. It had been one New Year's Eve full of serenity, light, colour.

Vera threw up on the carpet and made a long and pungent noise. It seemed like a deaf pain was grinding her body. Dana wasn't sleeping (even though it was past one o'clock at night) and suddenly got up. Claudia was sleeping, snoring annoyingly. 'I have to hang on. I will. The end will come. The end of pain and inability.'

Dana turned on the light, neared Vera, and, to her surprise, she was calm. There was vomit all over Vera's mouth and chin. She took a towel from the wardrobe and wiped it off, even though she felt really disgusted.

'You, miserable!'

Vera's mouth had contorted, her nose was running, and there were tears in her eyes.

'Why are you crying?', asked Dana, knowing that she won't get any answer. Vera was living in her own world.

"She is probably crying her fate. She'll die between these filthy walls, which were smelling of weakness and pain. But what about her, was she any different? Had she changed, was she another person, without any ghosts and depression? " I don't think that the gap is that deep."

Vera was crying so loudly that the walls were shaking.

"I am calm, I am calm", Dana kept repeating herself that and went out into the hallway, after a nurse. A magical pill would calm Vera down. The door at the surgery was closed, which meant that the nurse was sleeping.

'Open', said Dana, knocking firmly.

"Lazy women, who sleep at work."

A fat woman, with ruffled blonde hair, with eyes half asleep, stuck her head out of the door.

'Good morning', said Dana sarcastically.

'What do you want?', hummed the woman.

'A painkiller for Vera.'

'Where's the nurse?'

'Stop asking so many questions! A painkiller for Vera', Dana spat the words between her teeth.

The woman turned around and came back with a Diazepam.

'Give it to her, she'll sleep like a log.'

Dana looked at her ironically.

'You'll also sleep like a log, but without any pill.'

'Leave!', shouted the fat nurse. She lived among disabled people and life didn't offer her any joy.

Vera took the pill and fell asleep half an hour later. Dana lay in bed, but couldn't fall asleep. "Where's this nurse?" Just like that, a simple rhetorical question.

She got up and got out in the hallway. The nurses might have made a corner of their own somewhere, where they would drink coffee quietly or take a nap. But why did it count? She needed them. She sometimes hated them for their aggressive behaviour, although she knew that their salaries were very low and they were wiping the bottoms of some afflicted people. She would really like to smoke a cigarette. She went back to her room and took the pack of cigarettes by her bed. They were cheap, but useful. She got out in the hallway again, opened the window and lit one. She was wearing only a thin T-shirt and it seemed like the strong winter wind was blowing through her skin. She smoked slowly, deep in thought. Had she changed? She had been asking herself the same question. Had Eric changed her? Had the malice in her soul happen to suppress? Could her behaviour be just for show? Her feelings were confusing and she couldn't understand them. Was she happy, was she glad? She thought about it for a moment and then she concluded that she could be glad. And a part of her aggression seemed to have disappeared. She had read somewhere that raw, then polished aggression can push you to great achievements. It gives you the strength to go on. But it has limits. Sheer aggression, which sometimes reaches paroxysmal levels, can end lives.

No, she wasn't aggressive, but maybe with injustice. There had been a while, when she was so aggressive, paradoxically, a mild and ironic aggression. She liked seeing humility and aggression and she smiled to herself. But she wasn't glad. Depression appeared at night, uglier than death. She was glad now, of course. Maybe, who knows, happy. She had Eric, and that gave her strength. Eric had become her safety pole. It was remarkable. Eric was full of strength and life, in a place where negativity prevailed fiercely, he emanated light.

Was there really so much kindness in her soul, which had to come to surface? Had Eric managed to do that with an unprecedented courage? She inclined to believe that he had. The light was penetrating her heart, and she greeted it with effusion.

She smiled and smoked again.

She felt so much affection for Eric, but she didn't realise what kind of affection it was.

She was standing in the hallway, near the big window, with bars. She contemplated the night and exhaled the smoke through her nostrils. She felt good. She didn't think of anything now and she didn't impose this to herself either. Sometimes, she wanted badly that her thoughts didn't wander through her mind, finding tiresome answers. Now she was ALL RIGHT.

She finished smoking, opened the window a little and threw the cigarette butt away, which flew like a lonely firefly.

She wanted to leave, but his imposing stature made her stand still, like a stone. His eyes were glistening like two lanterns, which were throwing off frightening lightenings. Just like those of a crazy person.

Dana thought about it. She was brave, she had fought with many boys, but at the moment, she felt her entire being trembling. She didn't know whether from cold or from fright.

How come she had never thought about that, the fact that one of these lunatics could hurt her really badly?

Now, in the darkness of the night, she was standing face to face with a dangerous one. She had heard a lot about him and not quite pleasant things.

She could scream, but she didn't. She settled for a cold, transfigured by fear smile. Her palms became sticky and cold. She wiped them on her trousers, wih an automatic gesture. Beads of salty sweat invaded her forehead, just like sparkling dew beads.

'Jimmy!', she whispered, with a hoarse and faint voice. She could hear her own heart beating, like the rhythm of drums during the Inquisition. Back then, people were burnt on the pyre, there was the guillotine, there was death. Death was now, too. The thought itself made her have goose bumps.

The boy was slowly coming closer. He burped a little, like after a great meal. He clenched his yellow and decayed teeth.

A real monster, who was emanating a stinky sweat, with very shiny eyes, as if coming out of their sockets.

Dana didn't move from where she was standing. She seemed to have frozen. Even her own mind had frozen.

Jimmy rushed towards her like a true storm of madness. Her mind unfroze, enlivened.

Jimmy the lunatic will squash her just like that kind of insect with a greasy shell. A lot of colourful juice will come out. She will have her intestines out. Next, she also rushed towards him. She crashed into Jimmy's chest like a ship which wanted to break the fierce iceberg. A flood of punches were thrown close to the boy's neck, on his chest, where her eyes were expressing anger and despair at the same time. He was too strong, too crazy.

His punch knocked her down on the cold tile. Her

bright red blood gushed out of her lip and the brow bone got broken. She touched her face with trembling fingers. She thought for a moment. It's not always good to answer to aggression with aggression. In Jimmy's case, absolutely not. The girl felt her head whizzing, it was actually a strange sound, just like the one of a siren, which announced danger. The danger was real, it was next to her, so true that she felt like throwing up from fear. The blood drop was falling like an acid rain on the floor. Dana felt so helpless, so small that she felt like she was going to choke under Jimmy's big boots.

She showed a faint smile, more of a grimace.

'Jimmy, look...', she said, almost whispering, because she could no longer speak, 'I'll give you candies, sweets, anything you want, just leave me alone.'

His eyes looked like the cracks of a dry black ground. His face didn't show any sign that he had understood anything.

His face was bony and full of pimples with lots of pus... While she talked to him, he stood still, as if regrets engulfed him fiercely like in a fishing net.

The girl nodded, grinning, saying in silence, to herself, "That's it, you, fool, that's it, go, go away."

Jimmy stopped for a second, opened his mouth so as to smile, turned his head aside, and his saliva was trickling on his lips, shining. He suddenly turned around and ran down the stairs, screaming. She thought that his strangled voice was full of fear. Was Jimmy really aware of fear? Who knows?

Dana got up from the floor, touched her face slowly and had the strange sensation that it decomposed in an unusually rapid rhythm. She looked out of the window, through the iron bars, which seemed to chain up her being, making her vulnerable. The night was pitch black, just a few lights were lit, here and there, in the yard.

The young woman licked her lips and felt the metallic taste of blood. She went on contemplating the night. There weren't any mixed feelings, the anxiety that had monopolised for years wasn't palpitating, hate didn't triumph.

There was something going on with her, one thing, which her mind couldn't understand. She put her hand on her heart and felt how it was beating calmly and peacefully. She wasn't afraid anymore, now she felt good. She stretched her hand out and she felt the cold metal.

"Can you be happy in a prison?"

The bleeding had stopped, but it had curdled on the swollen lip, because she hadn't bothered to wipe it off. She went on feeling the pulse of the metal.

„If you want it, you can, or better said, if you have the power to float in freedom, it's the freedom you create for yourself, like a castle of cubes.'

Dana just stood for a few moments, without thinking about anything, then she went to the bathroom, finally she washed herself, looking at her face in the mirror. Her fingers were touching her skin slowly. She licked her lips again. With everything that had happened, she was smiling. A state of bliss was deforming her being, making her feel something indefinite. Maybe happiness? She wasn't too sure. It could be. Her thoughts were repeating, obsessively, the following question: "Can you be happy in a prison?"

'Can you be happy in a prison?'

The sun was shining brightly on them. Dana was sitting

on the stone bench, with those corners gnawed by time, and Eric in the wheelchair, next to her. The youngsters of the hospital hospice were passing by, playing with pebbles. A girl, who didn't seem to be older than 17, was struggling to remove a stone slab, to play with the sand under it. From time to time, her screaming seemed pretty much like the one of an Indian warrior.

Vera and Claudia were also outside, sitting on warm stones. A nurse had cut their hair, and they looked weird, a mixture of boy and girl, with bony faces, expressing helplessness.

Saliva was flowing out of Vera's mouth, through the fingers which she had stuck in the back of her throat. Dana glanced at her, then she went on looking at her own hands. She talked as if she were alone, in a nice place, with lots of greenery, trills of birds composing a symphony of nature. It was her alone, talking with her own thoughts.

At a certain moment, she nodded and raised her eyebrows as if betraying confusion.

'Can you be happy in a prison?', she said aloud.

Eric grabbed her hand and his wide open smile brightened his face.

'Are you with me now?'

The girl also smiled. She looked at him with big eyes, full of love.

'I'd never leave', she said touching the young man's chin with her her index finger.

'This gives me strength.'

'Really?'

'Do you doubt it?'

'Then, answer me.'

'Anything you want, honey. You can definitely be happy in a prison.'

She giggled.

'I knew it, I knew it.' She got up.

'Sit down', said Eric, but his voice sounded more of a prayer than of an order.

Her face expressed so much kindness that, for a second, he couldn't recognise her. His soul was suddenly filled with joy, bathing him in that blessed light, typical to fulfilment. He, Eric, the boy who had become a man, thanks to her, could easily consider himself an accomplished man. Accomplishments, thought the young man, can be of several kinds. Some strange, just like when compulsive, you become obsessive, wanting to break someone's heart or body, someone who provoked the ugly feeling of selfishness. Then you just want to hide your helplessness of being a human being. Others can be a source of life, a spiritual fulfilment, which helps you find yourself. It can be considered 'a source of life.' Was it too much to think that way? Wasn't he trying to exalt himself, assuming too much from God's work?

It's true, divinity had given him many chances, just like that, one after the other, which he did nothing but take them.

One day, bowing his head, in his chamber, in his wheelchair, he knew how to pull himself together, or he had just pulled himself together without much effort, he said a simple prayer, from his heart, "Lord, Jesus Christ, the Son of the Living God, have mercy on us."

That was it, but he had said, "have mercy on us", not "have mercy on me". She used to think only about herself. She repeated the prayer aloud and hearing her own words, she burst into tears of happiness. They were near God, and God was near them.

He was definitely an accomplished man. He had known how to save a person from going crazy, he had known how to give her LOVE.

He had definitely been a tool of God.

Dana sat on the stone bench. When she started talking, her voice seemed hoarse and faint.

'I knew it.'

'I believe you. Do you know why I've told you to sit down? Because this way you're closer to me and I can do this.'

He didn't seem clumsy when he grabbed her hands and took them to his lips, like a priceless treasure. Then, with the same simple warm gestures, he pulled her head gently and kissed her forehead, with a shudder of a blessed pleasure.

After that, she lifted her head and glanced at him with that look, much more different than that of the girl he had firstly seen. Back then, he could clearly understand her inner weakness, her sad and gloomy look, as if the sky above was flooded with clouds.

'Is it true that the clouds have just vanished?'

His question didn't take her by surprise, that was why she showed a faint smile in the corner of her lips.

'I hope so.'

'Is it too much for me to ask you this question? Is it something inapproapriate?'

The question wasn't inappropriate, he knew that, but he wanted to look like a saviour again. "I have drained the moor and irrigated your soul with the water of life." Who did he think he was? Anyway, he liked to think that he, Eric the Skinny, had done a good job, for her, the woman who would live forever, like a stigma, in his heart.

Dana kissed his lips, then his eyes so gently that they watered with excitement.

Then she held his head in her palms, and he shuddered with love and lust.

'Look into my eyes', she said, her look emanating that cold shadow of severity.

'It doesn't mean I am a perfect person. Trying to be perfect, that's sheer madness. I am bad, I am good, I am calm, I am nervous, I am beautiful, I am ugly.'

He laughed slowly, put her hands away, then continuing to hold them in his.

'You are the mark of duality in a person. But you've extirpated the poison. I've prayed a lot for this. You wanted to poison yourself so that you could curse the moment of nothingness and knock your head against all the walls.'

'I really wished the poison would flow inside me like a palpable poison, which could bring me the eternal sleep.'

He raised one hand in the air, as if wanting to stop a flow of negativity.

'We can contemplate the mornings bathed in light or the ones tired by grey mist, thinking of life. We are young, what more could we wish for? Nevertheless, life is a great gift from God.'

She looked at him for a moment of two, then turned back her head, as if she weren't interested in his words. But it wasn't like that. She was just looking, she was confident and full of hope.

Nina paid her a visit yesterday. She was accompanied by Bibi. She will forever be grateful to Bianca for the favour of bringing Nina here. Life was so clear and bright, Nina was so beautiful, with her angelic eyes. She'll always love her.

Then, she remembered Ms. Boobs' face clearly when she asked her for forgiveness from the bottom of her heart.

Bibi remained in a fierce frown. All the nurses at the centre said that "there", Dana would be completely exhausted and would go crazy. Dana had gone crazy indeed.

Bibi showed a stupid smile.

'Dana, err..'

'Just tell me that you forgive me, I know that I'm asking too much...'

Bibi felt lost.

'Dana, err..'

'Only if you can do this, Bibi.'

Bibi burst into a stupid laughter, which betrayed an immense emotion.

'What do you mean?', she finally asked.

Dana took a deep breath and said:

'Do you feel something for me, Bibi, do you hate me?'

'No', said the girl promptly. If she hated her? That is if she wanted to see her dead or punished?

'Dana', she said in a hesitant voice, 'I don't want you to die, nor do I want you to be punished.' "Although I wanted this once", she went on in silence.

Dana was crying, and so was Nina. It was a sudden joy.

Dana rushed towards Bibi and hugged her tightly. She knew that she forgave her when she felt her hug and her intermitent breath.

Bibi also told Dana, with tears in her eyes, that she, Nina and Micky lived in a social flat, but not since long ago. Who knows, maybe she'll sell her parents' house and they'll have their own money. "Had Ms. Boobs become so generous overnight?", thought Dana, then she decided not to agitate unpleasant thoughts.

Bibi also asked Dana when she would leave that place and pointed to the thick walls.

"Some day", answered Dana and asked her not to worry about her. She thanked her dearly that she looked after Nina.

"God, everything had changed indeed."

Dana suddenly got up and knelt in front of Eric, on the warm pavement, as if she started a saint prayer.

The boy's look was full of light, a shadow of astonishment on the background of a great joy. Her lips opened slowly, but she didn't say a word. Maybe it was too much for her to speak now.

'Do you accept me the way I am, baby?'

His joy turned into sheer happiness inside. Had she really considered him her boyfriend, from the bottom of her heart?

'But you, you...', he babbled, with his eyes full of tears, 'what do you see in me?'

She shook her head, shut up a little and then said:

'Love. You are able to give a lot of love, just immerse yourself in love. God has given you a lot of love.'

'Oh', he said, 'I'd like us to learn more about God, feel God, because God means a lot of love.'

She bent over even more and held his legs with her soft arms. She burst into tears and cried out loud for a while.

'My baby, my baby', she hummed, looking like the slave of a faded love.

He didn't say anything and let her unshackle.

Later on, Dana raised her head. Her face was wet with tears.

'Look', she said, with her voice strangled by a blessed emotion, pointing to the disabled youngsters, then to the thick walls of the building, 'the prison is not actually here.'

Then, her fingers clenched into a fist, with which she smote upon her chest.

'The prison is here.'

Eric once felt the taste of defeat, now he was feeling the taste of triumph.

'We have tried to get out, to build a new life in our own souls and we have succeeded. God help us.'

She nodded gladly.

'We have escaped, but even for a few seconds, we can be chained.'

'True, but only for a few seconds, just like you said.'

'Then what?'

'Then, we're free, baby.'

Printed in the United States
By Bookmasters